He put an arm around her shoulders and gave her a shake. "Hold on, Jenny. Don't go to pieces on me now. I'd really prefer that you keep on needling me. Remember what you were just saying. Tears aren't your style." He brushed a vagrant drop of water off her cheek, then bent over to kiss the spot tenderly. It was no journey at all from there to her lips.

A spontaneous antidote to the harrowing experience that they'd been through. But, for whatever reason, they found themselves kissing—passionately, ardently, frantically, desperately, and lengthily.

Also by Marian Devon
Published by Fawcett Books:

MISS ARMSTEAD WEARS BLACK GLOVES
MISS ROMNEY FLIES TOO HIGH
M'LADY RIDES FOR A FALL
SCANDAL BROTH
SIR SHAM
A QUESTION OF CLASS
ESCAPADE
FORTUNES OF THE HEART
MISS OSBORNE MISBEHAVES
LADY HARRIET TAKES CHARGE
MISTLETOE AND FOLLY

A SEASON FOR SCANDAL

Marian Devon

FAWCETT CREST • NEW YORK

A Fawcett Crest Book
Published by Ballantine Books
Copyright © 1992 by Marian Pope Rettke

Library of Congress Catalog Card Number: 91-92400

ISBN 0-449-22047-8

Manufactured in the United States of America

First Edition: July 1992

Chapter One

"**Y**OU LOOK LIKE the very devil!"

The Earl of Rexford glared at his only son, Lord Dalton.

Though many would have quarreled with the earl's assessment—Lord Dalton was generally considered one of the handsomest men in London—the fact that his extraordinarily blue eyes were bloodshot, his black hair was tousled, his unshaved cheeks were a trifle pallid, gave some credence to Lord Rexford's words.

"B'gad, Pierce"—he stamped the stick he carried upon the floor for emphasis, causing his suffering son to wince—"it's a disgrace to still be in your dressing gown at noon. When are you going to put a period to your carousing and set up your nursery?"

Lord Dalton sighed and collapsed in a wing-back chair that flanked an Adam fireplace. He waved a languid hand at its duplicate on the other side of the marble hearth. "Do sit down, Papa. If I'm to be harangued, let's at least be comfortable."

The older man yielded up his stick, gloves, beaver, and the greatcoat he'd worn against the February weather to the footman who had been lurking in the background since admitting him to his son's Mount Street residence. The servant thereupon disappeared, soon to return with a pot of strong, hot tea.

"Do you know, sir," Dalton remarked pleasantly after a sip of the restoring brew, "I suspect there are other ways to start a conversation than with inquiries about my matrimonial intentions, but damned if you've hit on an alternative for the last ten years."

"Can you blame me?" Lord Rexford's eyebrows were bushy, gray, and formidable when he frowned. "Neither of us is getting any younger."

"True. But since I'm not quite thirty yet, and you're only—err—fifty-something, I fail to see the need of all this urgency. As I think I've remarked each time we've had this conversation, if you're so concerned about the succession, why don't you remarry? I'm sure you're quite capable of producing other brats. Just look at you."

It was true that the Earl of Rexford did not look his fifty-seven years. And while not nearly as tall and never as good-looking as his only son, who owed both traits to his late mother's family, he was, by other standards, a fine figure of a man. He had retained his hair, a becoming iron-gray, and his waistline had expanded very little. He did require spectacles for reading, but since he was not addicted to that habit, it caused him little inconvenience. He could still spot the fox or the hare on the hunting field as quickly as the next cove.

His son acknowledged all this with an admiring look. "You really are looking quite fit, sir. Must be all that clean living and country air. I'll bet a monkey that all the Sussex widows are in hot pursuit.

So why haven't you remarried?" He'd dropped his bantering tone and was frankly curious.

His father, who had momentarily ceased to glare, resumed it. "You can seriously question why I haven't brought another female into my house? My God, Pierce; I never thought you lacked for common sense!"

Lord Dalton, who had four sisters still at home and two more now comfortably settled on nearby estates, acknowledged the hit. "I do see what you mean, sir."

"And as for starting up a nursery again—" Rexford shuddered. "I'd ask for much better odds than six to one for producing another male."

"Ah, breakfast." Lord Dalton welcomed the interruption as the footman reappeared with a heavily laden tray and set it down on a circular table at his elbow. "Never mind, Jack." He waved away the ministering servant. "We can manage."

There was an interlude while Lord Rexford heaped his plate with boiled eggs, ham, and Sally Lunn, while his slightly queasy son settled for a light wig. Then, "What brings you to London, sir?" Dalton inquired politely. "That is, besides your parental duty to periodically rake me over the coals."

"That's it," his lordship responded thickly as he chewed.

"Oh, come now." His son looked dubious. "You surely can't be serious. You wouldn't leave the hunting field on so feeble a pretext. For I can assure you, you've no need to vex yourself on my account. I do intend to wed—eventually."

"*Eventually* won't cut it, Pierce. Now's the time. Started to write you a letter about it, but knowing you as I do, I judged you'd just glance at the thing,

3

then pitch it in the fire. So I've made the trip here in person to tell you that—By the by"—another thought intruded—"do you have a voucher for Almack's?"

"Certainly." Lord Dalton looked slightly offended. While admittance to the Assembly Rooms in King Street, St. James, was jealously guarded by a cabal of patronesses who saw to it that only the crème de la crème of society attended, there could be no question of Lord Dalton's bona fides. "Not that I ever go there," he added. "For a more tedious way to waste an evening, I can't imagine."

"Well, you're going to start going. And to Fremantle House when you're asked there."

It had never fallen the Earl of Rexford's lot to order troops of soldiers into battle. But if the occasion had arisen, and he'd used the same tone he'd just employed, outgunned, outmanned companies would have unquestioningly moved forward into the very teeth of the enemy.

Lord Dalton was, however, made of sterner stuff. "Now why would I do a damn fool thing like that? For if there's any place likely to be an even bigger bore than Almack's, it's an establishment presided over by James Fremantle."

"I mean to tell you why if you'll keep your comments to yourself long enough to listen. Didn't I say I've come to London for that very purpose?" He placed his teacup on the hearth beside him and inched forward in his chair to give an urgency to what he was about to utter.

"Did I ever tell you about the Percival sisters, Pierce?" The question was rhetorical; Lord Rexford did not yield the floor. "It was the Season of '98, I collect. No, make that 1797. Twenty-one years ago

4

now. Fancy that." He did pause now to shake his head sadly and wonder at the passage of so much time.

"What about the sisters, sir?" his son prodded.

"Why, they took the town by storm. That's what about 'em. Four of them, there were. And all glorious. Nobody had ever seen four such lovely girls all in one package, as it were. And they hadn't a feather amongst 'em to fly with. Their father was a country parson, well connected, but poor as his own church mice. God knows how he raised the blunt for all of 'em to make their bows, but somehow he managed. And it paid off handsomely. Every last one of 'em married a fortune.

"Oh, did I mention that there was a pair of twins? The middle girls they were and alike as two peas in a pod." His face took on a dreamy quality. "I was in love with one of them."

His son, whose attention had wandered for a bit, was now all ears. "Oh, really? With just one, sir?"

"Of course just one!" his father snapped. "What do you take me for?"

"Well, you did say they were exactly alike. I just wondered how you told 'em apart, that's all. Are you quite sure they never pulled a switch on you? I've heard of twins getting up to that sort of thing. In point of fact, a friend of mine—"

"Devil take your friend!" his father interrupted. "Twins ain't the point here, you ninnyhammer."

"Well, then, what is?"

"The point is, these famous beauties now have three daughters who are about to make their bows." The earl looked expectantly at his offspring.

"Don't tell me. Triplets!"

"Don't be impertinent. Dammit all, I'm trying to

5

get it through your skull that this is the chance of a lifetime. And I'm—yes, by gad—*ordering* you to bestir yourself before the other beaux in town snap up the three of them. By gad, sir, I expect you to marry one of these girls."

"Even if they turn out to be antidotes?"

"They won't. The thing's impossible."

"Well, now, sir, I beg to differ. I've seen some perfect horrors whose mamas were, by all accounts, quite presentable in their salad days."

"Well you can rest easy on that score. Friend of mine saw Caro's daughter a few years back in Vienna. Turned out that Caro's husband's a diplomat. Surprised me no end. Never would have thought he had it in him. The daughter was only a schoolroom miss at the time, of course, but Cobb swore she'd outshine her mother. Not that I think that's possible. Bound to be an exaggeration. But still—"

"Caro? That was your twin, I take it."

"You might say that. Anyhow, it's her daughter I want you to marry."

"Sight unseen? Isn't that a bit rash? She could be a shrew or a sapskull, you know."

"Impossible."

"If you say so. By the by, did my mother know of—Caro?"

His father looked indignant. "Of course not. Wouldn't of been the thing to speak of it."

"Sorry."

This wasn't the time to ponder over his parents' marriage. They had always seemed content enough as he remembered. But their wedding had been arranged, he knew. A tradition his father seemed determined to continue.

"Isn't there a bit of incongruity here, though? I

mean to say, you've sat here telling me that you still regret letting the love of your life get away. And yet you want me to dangle after some chit you've picked out for me sight unseen. Where's my chance for a love match?"

"Well, if you've not managed the thing during these last ten years, I'd say it ain't likely to happen."

Lord Dalton's expression acknowledged the hit, and his father pushed home his advantage. "Besides, if you can't manage to fall head over heels with this particular diamond-of-the-first-water—well, there's something the matter with you, lad."

"If you say so."

Lord Dalton was feeling cornered. He made one last feeble attempt to fight his way out. "It still doesn't make sense to exert myself just because of a pack of sisters who were all the rage before The Flood. Why can't I do my own choosing in my own time, sir? I still can't share your sense of urgency."

The Earl of Rexford sighed. He'd anticipated this kind of opposition from his heir. Reluctantly he flung down his trump.

"Didn't want to have to say so, Pierce, but you leave me no choice. Went to see that London quack of mine yesterday. And not to put too fine a point on it—well, he told me I'd only a short time to live. Said I'd best be putting my affairs in order. And having you married, right and tight, Pierce, is the most pressing affair I can think of."

Chapter Two

THE HONORABLE JENNY Blythe paused on the threshold of her aunt's withdrawing room and struggled to hide her shock. When she had last seen her cousin, Lady Claire had been a plump, pretty child of ten. Now—and there was no other word for it—Claire was obese.

Jenny had just arrived. Her boxes were in the process of being removed from the traveling coach that had brought her to Grosvenor Square. Lady Fremantle's butler had informed her that whereas her ladyship and her cousin Sylvia were out shopping, her other cousin could be found practicing the pianoforte. Jenny had followed the sound of Mozart to its source.

In spite of the jolt her cousin's size had given her, she was forcibly struck by Claire's considerable musical skill. Consequently when Claire glanced up from her playing, the look that she encountered was fortunately admiring.

Claire's eyes in their turn widened. Well, now the shoe's on the other foot, Jenny thought, with wry amusement. "Bravo!" she said aloud. "That was marvelous."

"Jenny!" Lady Claire jumped up to give her cousin a welcoming hug. Jenny could not help but compare the embrace with being smothered by a bolster.

The cousins parted to gaze at each other affectionately. Though separated by too much distance to see each other often, they had been tireless correspondents. Jenny had always believed that there was little about Claire's life she did not know. Now she began to wonder.

But not for long. Her attention was suddenly distracted. "Well, well, well," she breathed as she gazed upward over her cousin's head. "There it is. The famous portrait. Well, well, well."

Followed by Claire, Jenny walked over to an ornate marble fireplace that occupied the center of a pale green, silk-covered wall. There above the mantle, dominating the drawing room, was an enormous painting.

Four young women, astonishingly beautiful, were artistically posed within a sylvan glade. They were draped in filmy gauze, each with a shoulder bare; the effect was vaguely reminiscent of Ancient Greece. One stroked a harp. Another, seated, held a flute carelessly on her lap. One bent studiously over a tambour frame, while the fourth appeared to be sketching the profile of the sister with the harp.

The two cousins stood silently for several moments, studying every aspect of the portrait. At last Jenny heaved a heartfelt sigh. "I hate to admit it, Claire, but they actually surpass all that I've ever heard. I always took the whole business with a grain of salt, you see."

"Did you really? I never did."

"Of course the artist—Romney, isn't it?—could have exaggerated."

"I really doubt it."

"But just what are they supposed to represent?"

"The Muses, I believe."

"Impossible. There were nine of them."

"The Graces, then?"

"Wrong number again. They were only three. Still, though, perhaps Sylvia's and my mother only count as one." She moved closer and studied the identical twins, whom the artist had treated as the focal point. "Yes, *Graces* most probably explains it."

"What they were were beauties." There was a tinge of bitterness in Claire's tone. "They didn't have to be anything else. By the by, our cousin Sylvia looks just like them."

"Well, so do you."

It was true. In a sense. Though almost obscured by cushions of fat, there were the same perfect features, the cornflower-blue eyes. Claire's hair was the identical softly curling blond of the portrait beauties. Her skin was fully as petal-fine.

"Oh, yes," she said wryly. "You could say that. You could even say that I'm twice the beauty they are. Three or four times even."

"Well, you're certainly closer to the ideal than I am," Jenny pointed out.

"That's not true. Why, you're"—Claire appeared to grope for the proper adjective—"stunning."

Her cousin laughed. "That's very good. Most people are stunned when they first see me."

"That's not what I meant at all and you know it. I'd give anything to look like you. You're so—"

"*Junoesque?* That's the word bookish folk use to describe me. Most, however, settle for Long Meg.

"No, let's face it, cousin, I've missed the famous Percival look by several miles. And I don't just refer to altitude. You're all so English-fair. And—well, just give me a tambourine and I could easily pass for your average gypsy."

The two cousins stared at the painting a little longer, and then, as if on cue, they began to giggle. The giggles increased to near-hysterical laughter.

"This really is absurd, you know," Jenny said as she wiped her streaming eyes. "What could those ninnys have been thinking of all those years ago? Fancy deciding that their daughters would make their come-outs together and repeat their triumph. Didn't it occur to the widgeons that some of us just might possibly look like our fathers?"

"I think they took it as some sort of sign when the three firstborn were so close in age and female."

They looked at each other once again, then back at the beauties—and were for the second time convulsed with laughter. "Well, thank God for Cousin Sylvia," Jenny choked. "She, at least, will uphold the family honor."

"You know," Claire remarked a bit later as she reclined on a Grecian couch in her cousin's bedchamber while Jenny arranged her toilet articles on the dressing table, "all that laughing has done me a world of good, but it actually isn't at all funny." She helped herself to another chocolate from the open box beside her. "In fact, I'd give all I own not to have to go through with this business."

"The come-out? Now you're being absurd. You simply have to forget all that nonsense about comparing us to our mothers."

"Easy enough to say. But will anyone let us? I've been here for two whole days and Aunt Lydia still has a fit of the vapors every time she claps eyes on me. She keeps moaning, 'How could my sister allow her only daughter to get so fat?' "

"Well, that's Aunt Lydia's problem. I, for one, am quite willing to put up with all sorts of nonsense in order to enjoy the freedom of a London holiday. It's obvious that you don't have a gaggle of younger brothers and sisters to look after the way I have or you'd welcome the chance to spread your wings and see something of the world."

"I wish I did have a gaggle of sisters." Claire swallowed her chocolate and popped in another. "Then Mama would not have to be quite so disappointed in me."

Jenny paused in her search for a mislaid hairbrush to give her cousin an anxious look. She was disturbed by Claire's obvious unhappiness and appalled by her ravenous chocolate consumption. It was all she could do not to point out the obvious: If Claire was unhappy with her size, her behavior could only make things worse.

Instead, she gave her cousin an affectionate look and went to sit beside her. "Come now"—she patted the plump hand—"you're making a Cheltenham tragedy out of something that could really be fun."

"For you, perhaps. You've no reason to dread the come-out. Once people get over the fact that you're not cut from the same pattern card as the previous generation, why, you'll have no end of gentlemen dangling after you. You're every bit as pretty as the famous Percivals, you know."

"What a rapper," her cousin said, laughing. "But I do appreciate your loyalty."

"No, it's true. You have much more—more . . ."

"Height?"

"No, peagoose," the other said, giggling. "I think

character is the word I'm groping for. You look more
. . . interesting. Oh, you'll have no trouble at all in
catching a husband, Jenny."

"No, that's where you're wrong. I know from sad
experience that gentlemen are not comfortable with
a female who towers above them. And as for flirt-
ing—well, that's quite beyond me. Batting one's
eyelashes down at the top of a man's head can never
have the same effect as batting them up at him.

"But never mind. I don't have my heart set on
catching a husband. What I really want to do is see
the metropolis—the Tower, the museums, Westminster Abbey—Oh, all of it. I can hardly wait."

"Well," Claire observed glumly, "we'll need escorts for most of that."

"That shouldn't present a problem. If our cousin
is half as lovely as you say, we'll just stake her out
like a Judas goat and have her admirers squire all
of us here and there."

"Oh, you are a goose!" Claire laughed, carefully
choosing another of the rapidly diminishing chocolates and, after an exploratory nibble, returning it
to the box to take another. "Let's just hope our
cousin Sylvia is generous with her beaux."

"By the by, what's she like? Besides the obvious,
I mean to say. What's Sylvia really like? Good
heavens, that sounds like Shakespeare's verse,
doesn't it? 'Who is Sylvia? What is she? That all
our swains commend her'?"

Claire looked thoughtful as she closed the chocolate box on the one remaining piece. "I don't think
I can really say. For we haven't become at all acquainted. We've never sat down for a coze or anything like that.

"I will say one thing, she was quite embarrassed
13

over the fuss our aunt made over her. I'd arrived first, don't you see"—Claire grimaced—"and I'm sure Aunt Lydia was braced for the worst. So Cousin Sylvia proved to be an answer to prayer. Aunt all but fawned over her, and I collect that made our cousin quite uncomfortable. For my sake, that is. But that's just a feeling. As I said, we've never actually talked together or anything like that. She's very—quiet."

"Shy, perhaps?"

"Oh, I shouldn't think so. I cannot imagine what she could find to be shy about. But somehow I got the impression—But, no, that's fanciful. I've nothing really to go on."

"Come on," Jenny prodded. "Out with it. What's your impression?"

"Well, no. The more I think on it, it's too absurd."

"Oh, do tell. I don't plan to carve your words in stone, you know. We can agree later that you're most likely mistaken, but what is your impression?"

"Well, if I didn't know better—for there's not the least doubt in my mind that our cousin Sylvia will be the belle of every ball that she attends . . . But if it were not for that, I'd say that she is dreading the come-out almost as much as I am."

"Indeed?" Jenny's eyebrows rose in surprise. "Would you care to elaborate? Just what gives you—?" She cut off her words at the sound of approaching voices while Claire quickly stuffed her chocolate box behind the cushion of the couch. A light tap on the door preceded its opening. A modish-looking woman and a petite young beauty entered the room.

Thanks to a talented modiste, an abigail with a flair for hair arrangement, and her own good figure, Lady Fremantle still held considerable claim to beauty. She was, however, cast entirely in the shade by the young woman who trailed after her. For Lady Sylvia Kinnard, so her cousin Jenny thought, might have just stepped out of the Romney portrait.

Jenny wrested her attention away from Sylvia and stood to greet her aunt. This action had the effect of freezing Lady Fremantle in her tracks. The dowager looked appalled. She threw her hands up in the air. "Don't tell me you are my other niece!" she gasped. "Heaven preserve us! You *are* a Long Meg!"

Chapter Three

DINNER WAS, TO say the least, a strained affair. Jenny, who kept country hours at home, had thought she'd never last till seven. She took her seat in the sumptuous dining room and gazed ravenously around her at the bounty. Harricot of mutton, neck of venison, a sauté of sweetbreads and mushrooms dominated the first remove. It was all she could do to force herself to take genteel portions of the dishes next to her, and she ate her first few bites of venison and sweet peas with unalloyed pleasure. But then she noticed the plate of biscuits and the glass of water being set before her cousin Claire and her appetite deserted.

Lady Fremantle, seated at the foot of the table pulling apart a pheasant with apparent relish, saw her distressed look. "I have persuaded Claire to eat as little as possible between now and her debut into Society. Granted, a week is not much time to undo the damage of what I can only term unbridled gluttony, but it is a beginning."

"Surely," Jenny protested as Claire's face flamed red, "she needs more than biscuits and water."

"I am merely following the regime that served Lord Byron so well when he began to put on unde-

16

sirable weight," her aunt replied in a tone that pronounced the matter closed.

"I hardly consider Byron a proper model to be followed in this household," her stepson remarked dryly from his place at the table's head. Jenny hoped that he would follow up this observation by overruling her aunt's decision, but he did not.

It was not in Lord Fremantle's nature to lock horns with his stepmama. He had been only five when she had captivated his widowed father at the famous come-out. The new Lady Fremantle had not been the maternal sort and had left the rearing of the lonely little boy to those hired to do so. She had never been unkind, however, and his lordship, after he came of age, was reasonably content to have her run his household.

He was a quiet, self-contained young man, uninterested in the social milieu of his stepmama. This suited Lady Fremantle well, since she had no desire to be supplanted by a daughter-in-law and had managed, in fact, to dampen the aspirations of several ambitious mamas who would have thrown their daughters at his head for his considerable fortune. And since he was not blessed with romantic, Byronic good looks, being instead thirtyish, with thinning, mouse-colored hair, pale blue eyes, and a countenance neither displeasing nor noticeable, the daughters themselves made no great push in his direction.

Despite his general disapproval of the social scene, Lord Fremantle had raised no objection to sponsoring his stepcousins' come-out. Nor was he lacking in social skills himself, as he now demonstrated by diverting the attention away from his

17

humiliated cousin Claire. "And how did you leave your family, Cousin Jenny?"

"On the whole, quite well," she replied, a little too heartily to cover the general embarrassment. "Of course, with a brood like ours, there's always something amiss, you realize. Just before I left, Charles, our seven-year-old, fell out of the apple tree and sprained his wrist rather badly. But he was so proud of the sling he wore that it took away the pain. He went around for the rest of the day being a casualty of Waterloo."

Lord Fremantle chuckled dutifully, and Lady Sylvia, who had hardly spoken throughout the meal, was also moved to help ease the tension. "Just how many brothers and sisters do you have, cousin? Oh, dear. I really should know that, shouldn't I?" She looked embarrassed. "But living abroad, and all . . ."

"Oh, no need to apologize. I own I sometimes lose track myself. But at last count there were eight of us."

"And what your mama could be thinking of to have another I cannot imagine," Lady Fremantle chimed in crossly. "She could not have chosen a worse time to become enceinte—again."

It was on the tip of Jenny's tongue to observe that surely her papa must share the blame, but she bit the words back as perhaps too indelicate. "Mama was most sorry not to be able to come to London with me," she substituted. "But our doctor told her it would be quite unwise."

"Well, she would have been of little use in her condition anyhow," her ladyship grumbled as she helped herself to fruit and cheese. "But I must say it was the outside of enough. When we planned your come-out years ago, it was agreed that all four of the Percival sisters would take part. We had hoped to make it a re-creation, as it were, of our own Season. And how it should have come about that I, the only childless one of the four, should have full charge—not that I'm not pleased to do so," she added as her nieces exchanged furtive glances. "But I had looked forward to a reunion with my sisters." She sighed theatrically. "It's been years now since we were together. Really, Jenny, it was too bad of your mother to be so inconsiderate. And as for your mother, Claire, I suppose it's understandable that she would not wish to come to London."

Jenny had thought it impossible for her cousin to look more miserable. But at her aunt's tactless remark, Claire appeared ready to sink right through the floor. Lord Fremantle cleared his throat, apparently about to change the subject, but her ladyship plowed on.

"As for Louisa"—she turned to Sylvia—"I really cannot see why she did not come with you. She has not the slightest excuse for failing to do so. And I should have thought that nothing in the world would have prevented her—" Her words were superseded by her shock as Lady Sylvia suddenly burst into tears, jumped to her feet, muttered, "Pray excuse me," and fled the room.

The remaining diners sat in stunned silence. Lady Fremantle recovered first. "Well, really!" she exclaimed.

"Perhaps I should go after her," Jenny offered.

"It might be wise to give her some moments to collect herself," Lord Fremantle reflected. "I expect that the long journey, plus the excitement of a London Season, are proving to be a great strain on her nerves."

"Well she's too sensitive by half if she took offense at anything I said." Lady Fremantle helped herself to tart.

At the conclusion of the meal, Claire pleaded the headache and fled to her room, and to her hoard of chocolates, her cousin feared. This left only Jenny to spend a dutiful hour and a half in the withdrawing room with her aunt, after which she got no argument when she proposed an early night.

But once she'd made her escape, she was in a quandary over which of her distressed cousins needed her the most. Well, at least she knew what to do for Claire, whereas her cousin Sylvia was an enigma. So, making sure her aunt was nowhere in sight, she stole down the back stairs to the kitchen.

Jenny found the servants grouped around the table at their own supper and was much embarrassed when they all sprang to their feet. "Oh, pray don't let me disturb you. I was feeling rather peckish, you see." Her face grew pink as she recalled the bounty of the dining table—which had been followed later on by a laden tea tray. "I'll just help myself to a little something." She had spied the joint and turkey, flanked by an array of vegetables, laid out on the dresser.

She was joined, however, by Mrs. O'Hara, the cook, who was surprisingly young and slim for such a culinary artist. "I'm sure you're welcome to whatever you see, miss," she said in a low voice. "But if it's Lady Claire you're concerned with, His Lordship has already seen to that. I sent up a tray just a bit ago. But His Lordship did ask, miss, that we not mention the fact to Her Ladyship."

20

"My lips are sealed," Jenny whispered back. "How very kind of his lordship."

"He is a most considerate gentleman," the cook replied as she carved off a thick slice of beef and placed it between two pieces of bread, then wrapped it in a napkin. "Best take this along for yourself, miss. As an excuse like. We didn't see the need to let the entire staff know, you see, that we were going against Her Ladyship's precise orders."

"Oh, yes, I do see," Jenny replied conspiratorially. Then she added in a louder voice, "Thank you very much, Mrs. O'Hara. This will be the very thing to help me sleep well."

She stole back up the stairs, feeling rather like one of the spies she often represented in her younger brothers' games, and tapped softly on Claire's bedchamber door.

There was a long delay, during which she thought she heard the rattle of dishes. "It's me, Jenny," she hissed through the heavy paneling.

"You should have said so," Claire said reproachfully after she'd unbolted the door, then relocked it. "I thought you were Aunt Lydia."

"Sorry. I should have realized. I went to fetch you supper, but Cook told me that our cousin James had seen to it already."

She watched with fascination as Claire knelt to pull a heavy tray out from under the bed ruffle. It made her wonder what else might be concealed there.

"Wasn't this kind of our cousin?" Claire's eyes moistened as she sat down on the couch with the tray in her lap. "And brave. I don't know how he has the courage to go against Aunt Lydia's orders."

"Well, it is his house." Jenny pulled the dressing-

21

table chair nearer her cousin. "Besides, our aunt will most probably never know. I do believe that the servants are very much in his lordship's pocket."

"Even so, it was exceedingly good of him. I would not have expected such kindness."

Jenny looked at her cousin thoughtfully while Claire gnawed at a chicken wing. She rather suspected that kindness had been a short commodity in that young lady's life.

"Won't you have something?" Claire inquired politely as she helped herself to pickled beets. "There's certainly enough here for the both of us."

That was true, Jenny observed, as she politely declined the offer. The quantity was certainly not lacking. But she also noticed that someone seemed to have selected the food quite carefully. Lean meats and vegetables predominated, with fruit and cheese to follow. Certainly a far more wholesome diet than the ubiquitous chocolates.

"Tell me, Claire . . . what did you make of our cousin Sylvia's outburst?" Jenny asked when the other had devoured the last crumb.

"I don't know what to make of it." Claire wiped the chicken grease from her fingers with a linen serviette. "But I was right, was I not? She doesn't want to be here in the least. I can't begin to imagine why, but there it is."

"Do you think we should go see about her?"

"I think that *you* should go see about her."

"She's your cousin, too."

"Yes, but I scarcely know her."

"Well, you're as well acquainted as I am."

"But you're much better at that sort of thing than

22

I am, Jenny. Comes of having all those younger siblings, I don't doubt."

Jenny gave an exasperated sigh and stood up. "Fustian. My own mother says that I'm totally devoid of tact. But somebody ought to look in on the girl. And better me than our aunt—speaking of tact.

"Well, good night, Claire. Sweet dreams." She leaned over and gave her cousin's plump cheek a peck.

"Do tell our cousin that I'm worried, too. I truly am, you know. It's just that I wouldn't know what I should say."

"Well, fools rush in. I'll see you in the morning, Claire."

But when Jenny tapped softly on Lady Sylvia's door, there was no reply. She opened the door a crack and saw by the moonlight streaming in the window that her cousin had already gone to bed. "Cousin Sylvia, are you asleep?" she called softly.

The only answer was a slow, rhythmic breathing.

There was no good reason for it, but even though Jenny gently closed the door again, she was quite convinced that her cousin Sylvia was wide awake.

Chapter Four

"I'LL TAKE THAT one."

The Honorable Jenny Blythe, accompanied by her cousins and chaperoned by Lady Fremantle and her stepson, stood in the ballroom doorway scanning the members of the ton packed together for a Wednesday night Assembly at Almack's. Her eyes had settled upon a distinguished, rather bored-looking gentleman who towered above the crush. Both her cousins, who had been viewing the Assembly Room with approximately the same enthusiasm they might exhibit if mounting the platform steps to the guillotine, giggled. "It doesn't work like that, peagoose," Claire whispered. "*They* pick us."

"Really? Well, what a poor arrangement."

"This is no time for funning, Jenny," her aunt scolded in an aside. At the same time, aware that they were rapidly becoming the center of everyone's attention as one clique after another spied them to turn and nudge and whisper to their neighbors, she managed to keep a fixed smile upon her face. "You must learn to curb your unfortunate tendency toward levity. It's most unbecoming. And as for the gentleman you've just singled out, no need to set your cap in that direction. That's Lord Dalton. The most sought-after bachelor in town. He's eluded all pursuit for ages. Indeed, miss, you aim too high."

"Well, a person of my stature has to aim high, Aunt," Jenny replied, sotto voce, with a perfectly straight face. "Never mind what the rest of the world sees in Lord Dalton. I'm attracted by the fact that he's the tallest man in the room."

Claire and Sylvia laughed again, bringing on another well-hidden scold. As she nodded to first one acquaintance and then another, Lady Fremantle's ostrich feathers bobbed above a cluster of curls that were definitely unmatronlike. Her smile never wavered while she whispered to her nieces, "Get control of yourselves, young ladies. I cannot stress sufficiently the importance of this evening."

Actually she had no further need to do so. She had done nothing else for the past week as she endeavored to prepare her nieces for their entrée into society. And, all things considered, she had done her best. No one could do more. She barely suppressed a shudder as she heard, or imagined, the gasps and titters elicited by the sight of her two outsized protégées.

Well, at least no one could say they were not dressed suitably. She had Sylvia to thank for that, her ladyship conceded.

Indeed, Lady Sylvia had demonstrated a decided flair for fashion. She had overridden her aunt's determination to deck out her cousins in gowns becoming to the paragons in the Romney portrait. She had insisted upon a simple round dress for Claire, Urling's net over a soft gray slip. And with a firmness that amazed her relatives and made them wonder if they'd only imagined her still-unexplained flood of tears and sudden exit from the dining table, she had vetoed the lace flounces festooned with bouquets of roses and bluebells that the French modiste had insisted upon, substituting for them a tiny, twisted rouleau of satin and pearls.

Even the strong-minded Jenny had listened meekly to Sylvia's advice. She was wearing a white crepe gown with a three-quarter-length apron, which, coupled with the several bands of silk tassels that finished off the skirt, distracted the eye from the exaggerated length of the current high-waisted fashion.

Every eye seemed fixed upon the second-generation Percivals. Lord Dalton was no exception. From across the room he experienced a surprising twinge of disappointment. He could have sworn that he hadn't taken his father's raptures seriously, but there it was again, that familiar sense of letdown he always felt when someone had promised to produce the "perfect girl" for him.

"Oh, I say," a voice at his elbow remarked. He looked down to see young Reginald York-Jones, a fellow member of White's Club for Gentlemen and Lord Rexford's godson, staring in the same direction. "That can't possibly be the Percival offspring, can it?"

"Must be. They're with Fremantle, their stepcousin."

"Well, that's what I get for being bear-led by my father," York-Jones sighed. "Had a letter from the old fossil practically ordering me to dance attendance."

"You too, eh?" Dalton grinned.

"Oh, lord, yes. He made it sound like multiples of Venus were bound to appear. *Oddities* would be more like it."

"Oh, you're coming it a bit strong, aren't you? Granted they don't live up to their advance publicity, but except for being such a Long Meg, the dark one's not bad."

"Easy enough for you to say." The diminutive York-Jones looked up—and up—at his lordship. "You've no need to be put off by trees. And I suppose you'll also add that except for looking like a fleecy cloud bank, the other one—Oh, my word!" He broke off with a sharp intake of breath as Lady Sylvia Kinnard moved out from behind her corpulent cousin to be presented to the Almack's patronesses. "Now that's more the thing, I'd say."

Lord Dalton silently echoed the other's sentiments as he, too, stared at the vision that had suddenly materialized. Lady Sylvia seemed ethereal, gowned in white lace over white satin. The high waistline accented her perfect bust. Her creamy throat was bare, as were her shoulders, except for the tiniest of puffed sleeves decorated with knots of pale blue ribbon. Satin cockleshells of the same blue color accented a narrow lace flounce that allowed the merest glimpse of her trim, ribbon-laced ankles and white satin shoes. Her hair was dressed in the French fashion, swept up to the crown and entwined with tiny white roses. Soft golden curls escaped to frame her face.

"She's—an—angel" the Honorable Reginald stuttered. "Looks like my hoary sire didn't exaggerate after all."

"Mine did," Lord Dalton drawled. "He led me to expect three of those. Excuse me, Reggie." He moved purposefully off to find a patroness who could introduce him to this vision.

Lord Dalton was not accustomed to being second

27

best. But it took time to disengage Lady Cowper, the most amiable of the seven ladies in authority, from a whispered conversation concerning the latest royal scandal. Then the patroness would keep pausing to speak to this person and that as they made their way across the ballroom. So by the time they reached the chairs where Lady Fremantle had seated her charges, two other chaperons were there before them with swains in tow. Lady Sylvia was instantly engaged for the cotillion. Sizing up the situation, literally, Lady Cowper quickly presented Lord Dalton to the Honorable Jenny Blythe, leaving Lady Claire to the much shorter foot-guard captain.

"See, what did I tell you about our own Judas goat?" Jenny whispered to Claire as they rose to join their partners.

After they'd taken their places in the forming set, Jenny stole a glance at her partner, noting as she did so that it was refreshing to look upward for a change. This pleasant reflection soon turned to pique. His eyes were fixed upon her cousin Sylvia across the room. Squelching the urge to administer a swift kick, she cleared her throat delicately when the dance demanded their participation. Lord Dalton danced easily and gracefully for a gentleman of his stature, she observed. As a matter of fact, so did she. But she did not think for one minute that he noticed. After they'd completed the figure, they went back to their original occupations. He stared at Lady Sylvia; she looked at him.

But she could find nothing to read in his expression. He seemed almost scientifically detached as he silently watched her cousin's every move. Well, two can play that game, Jenny decided, and matched his silence with her own. But since he was unaware of her forbearance, this ploy left much to be desired. She went on the attack.

"It's your turn to say something now, Mr. Darcy. I talked about the dance, and you ought to make some kind of remark on the size of the room or the number of couples."

"Eh?" He shifted his attention, but looked at her without interest. "I think you're a bit confused, Miss Blythe. I'm Dalton, not—err—Darcy."

"Not really confused, your lordship. Actually I was quoting from a favorite book of mine—where the heroine also had a partner who wouldn't bother to do the polite."

"Oh, I see." He smiled frostily. "And did the gentleman in question grow immediately loquacious?"

"Sufficiently to make it through the set, as I recall."

"Well, then, I can do no less. How's this? Tell me about your cousin."

"With pleasure. Besides being blessed with amiability, Claire is remarkably talented. Musically, I mean. She plays the pianoforte skillfully, but her real forte is singing. She has a voice like an angel."

"Claire? I thought her name was Sylvia." He looked momentarily puzzled. "Oh. I see."

She threw up her hands in mock surprise and seized the opportunity to bat her eyelids upward. (It was disappointing to discover that this felt quite as silly as the other way around.) "Oh, stupid me! I had no idea that you meant my *other* cousin—the one you've been watching like a hawk all evening. Well, then. Actually I don't know Sylvia very well at all. She has always lived abroad, you see. But I can say that she is very"—she felt a necessity to stress the word—"*nice*. And she's rather quiet. Shy, I suspect."

"Hardly a family trait, I take it?"

Jenny chose to ignore the hit. She continued her summation. "And she's breathtakingly lovely. But then you may have noticed that. However, I think you're a bit—old, for her."

He looked down his nose. "Hardly, I collect. I'm not yet thirty."

"Oh, no? Well, you could have fooled me. But then I expect that London gentlemen are rather more world-weary than our country types."

"Town-bronze may not necessarily be a virtue, Miss Blythe, but I never heard that it made one old before his time. As for your cousin's and my relative ages, I've always heard it was advantageous in a marriage for a man to be more mature."

"You do jump ahead, don't you?" She looked at him curiously. "Shouldn't you at least meet my cousin before posting the banns?"

"I was merely being hypothetical. Trying to refute your premise that I was too ancient for your cousin."

"Oh, well," Jenny sighed. "You waste your time, for I didn't really mean it. I was going to say that you're too *tall* for her, but I thought that observation would come better from another source."

"I see. And I am, I collect, just right for you."

"In inches, yes. Though it doesn't appear we'd suit in any other way."

"Nor in that." He was finding this pert miss a bit tiresome. "At least I've no desire to sire a whole new race of giants."

They were separated again by the demands of the dance. This was just as well, for as much as Jenny longed to wither his lordship with a scathing set-down, nothing sprang to mind. He, on the other hand, had no such handicap. "May I give you a word of advice, Miss Blythe?" he asked when they came back together."

"Why seek permission? It's obvious that you're about to."

"Here goes then. You've come to town much heralded, because of your famous mother and aunts. And since you're not at all in the style of those fabled creatures, it's obvious that you've decided to make yourself noticed by your clever tongue."

"I can assure your lordship"—Jenny's black eyes took on a dangerous glint—"that since the age of twelve I've never had to work at being noticed. That distinction was accorded me automatically."

"And I can assure you, Miss Blythe, that you cannot hope to succeed in London Society by impertinence. What might get you favorable notice in provincial Society will be more likely to disgust the more jaded members of the ton. We've seen it all, you see, Miss Blythe. And your attempts to be noticed can never hope to rival those of a Lady Caroline Lamb, for instance. So perhaps instead of aping the heroine of your favorite novel, who sounds rather tiresome, by the by, you would do better to emulate your cousin. The quiet—or shy—one, I mean."

"And you, sir, should consider taking orders. Then your bent for sermonizing would have a captive audience. I, at least, am now let off the hook."

The orchestra's final note had faded away. Jenny's eyes blazed as she returned a token curtsy to his perfunctory bow.

Chapter Five

LADY CLAIRE WAS fully as relieved as her cousin that the dance was coming to a close. Though her partner, the reluctant military man, was more at pains than Lord Dalton to do the polite, his attention had also kept straying toward Lady Sylvia. He, too, had some difficulty in disguising his relief when the set at last was ended.

Settled once again in her chair beneath the orchestra balcony, Claire was wondering if it might not be possible to slip away to the cloakroom while her aunt was engaged in a rehash of past glories with a bored contemporary. Just as she saw her chance and had halfway risen, a deep voice asked, "May I have the honor of this dance, Lady Claire?"

"Oh." She switched her gaze from Lady Fremantle to find her stepcousin looming solemnly over her. You don't really have to do this, you know, she longed to say, but quickly changed her mind. It would no doubt distress Lord Fremantle to have his motives questioned. She gave him a timid smile instead and took the arm he offered.

She did not entirely abandon her impulse toward plain speaking, however. "I've had no opportunity to thank you for your kindness, Lord Fremantle," she told him when they'd reached a point in the country dance that called for no participation on their part.

"Eh?" He obviously had no notion of what she meant.

She lowered her voice so the neighboring couples might not hear. "I was given to understand that you were responsible for having my meals served in my room."

"Oh, that. Well, yes." He looked embarrassed. "You mustn't think, Lady Claire, that I'm in the habit of countermanding your aunt's orders. It's only on rare occasions that I think she lacks good judgment. And then I find it's simpler to have a quiet word with the servants rather than a head-on confrontation with my stepmama. For I've learned she soon gets over these little crochets."

Claire sighed. "I don't think she will soon get over her shock at the sight of me. It's understandable that she'd wish to reduce me as quickly as possible."

"Not at the expense of your health." His lordship frowned. "May I speak frankly, Lady Claire?"

"Of course, Lord Fremantle."

"At the risk of giving you the wrong impression—for I can sincerely say that I've never personally had the slightest cause to complain of my stepmama's treatment—you must not take her criticisms too much to heart. She is, in certain respects, a very shallow woman."

At this moment they were swept apart by the dance. Claire felt almost lighthearted as she was led through a figure by another gentleman who concluded that the Beauty's daughter, while several stone too heavy for his liking, seemed a jolly enough sort.

When she once more joined her partner, Claire was loath to let the subject die. "How old were you," she asked, "when your father remarried?"

"Five."

"That must have been a difficult time for you."

He seemed to think it over seriously. "No, not really," he concluded. "Though I collect it might have been otherwise had I been a girl."

"Oh, really? Why?"

"Well, for one thing, I would have had to look forward to all of this." His eyes swept the ballroom with disapproval. "I must say, Lady Claire, that you ladies have my utmost admiration for your courage. I'd as lief ride into battle, I do believe, as to be flung into Society, willy-nilly, in this fashion. It's rather like the Persian slave bazaar, wouldn't you say?"

She laughed. "There is a certain similarity now you mention it. Still"—she sobered up—"it wouldn't be quite so bad if one didn't have quite so much to live up to."

"The fabulous Percival sisters?"

"Well, your mother does tend to go on and on about her come-out, doesn't she?"

"Indeed I was raised upon the story. It quite eclipsed Cinderella and The Sleeping Beauty, I must say. I collect," Lord Fremantle considered, "that on the whole it was a very good thing my stepmama never had a daughter."

"Well, at least she has my cousin Sylvia. This evening appears to be a triumph for her." Claire had not failed to notice the line of suitors who besieged the Beauty for every dance.

"That's true." Lord Fremantle followed her gaze. Lady Sylvia had just joined hands with Lord Dalton and the two were going down the set. "She has hitherto seemed refreshingly unconscious of her great beauty. I've admired her for it. I hope that this evening—and my stepmama—will not spoil her."

For some unaccountable reason, Lady Claire's spirits had began to plummet once again. She thought it a good thing on the whole that the dance had now concluded.

Lord Dalton's frame of mind was not much better. He took note of Lady Sylvia's mechanical smile as he thanked her for the dance. And even though she readily agreed to stand up with him again later in the evening, he could detect nothing beyond social civility in her acquiescence. He was more than a trifle out of sorts as he went to lounge against the wall. His masklike expression effectively concealed a mood that came close to a fit of the sulks.

Lord Dalton was not at all accustomed to female indifference. Indeed, his chief problem with the fairer sex had been the need to ward off too much attention. Take the Beauty's forward cousin, for instance.

Dalton inwardly cursed himself. Why he'd allowed that treelike chit to irritate him was beyond his understanding. A chilly setdown was more his style. No, not even that. He was wont to squelch pretensions with a haughty stare, coupled, if the occasion seemed to warrant extreme measures, with the elevation of an eyebrow. And yet he'd given that tiresome young woman a scold that he'd not even have wasted on his bothersome sisters. He felt his dignity had been diminished by the exchange.

Dammit, her remark about sermonizing had hit home.

Still, though, he realized he would not ordinarily give a second thought to their conversation. It was not the Percival sisters' offspring, per se, that were ruffling his feathers. It was the situation. Though well aware of his duty (he shuddered inwardly at the ominous word), he had felt no sense of urgency about marriage until his father's visit. Indeed, few men were more content than his lordship with the bachelor existence. True, the age of thirty loomed rather large. But even that milestone had aroused no panic in his breast. His father's announcement had, however, been a facer.

Even though they'd never been particularly close, Dalton did have, he now realized, a considerable affection for his parent. And if it was his father's wish to see his son settled before he shuffled off this mortal coil, then, by George, he'd do it. And since his had always been of an "in for a penny, in for a pound" disposition, he was determined to marry his father's choice. He just wished that Lady Sylvia were more receptive. Dammit, marriage was bad enough. He was in no mood to woo—

"Good God, Dalton! You here at Almack's!" A drawling voice at his elbow interrupted his lordship's reverie. "I'd as soon expect to see our Prinny walk the high wire."

Dalton turned to find Mr. Roderick Chalgrove eyeing him with a languidly bored expression, seemingly the only expression of which Mr. Chalgrove was capable.

He was a handsome man, of medium height, fair, with shrewd gray eyes framed by dark, heavy lashes. His sartorial elegance and jaded manner were aped by many a young aspirant to fashion. The dandy had been on the town as long as Dalton. They belonged to the same clubs and ignored the same invitations. They had known each other far too long to even consider whether they were friends.

"Chalgrove." Dalton acknowledged the other's greeting with a mocking bow. "I'd say it was stranger to find you here than me. Looking over the latest crop of husband-hopefuls are you?"

"Why, yes, as a matter of fact." The dandy extracted an enameled snuffbox from the recesses of his coat, placed some of the contents upon his wrist, and inhaled delicately. (Several young men nearby covertly eyed this maneuver and vowed to practice the elegant gestures later on in the privacy of their rooms.) "I'm here by royal command you could say. My uncle's, not Farmer George's."

Mr. Chalgrove did not need to explain that his uncle was the one piper who could call the tune in his care-for-nothing nephew's life anytime he wished. Dalton was well aware that Chalgrove was heir to the uncle's immense fortune.

"Don't tell me," his lordship groaned. "The Percival sisters."

"*Et tu*, then?"

"Oh, lord, yes. Seems my father was badly smitten a quarter of a century ago."

"So was that entire generation, it appears. Well, let's get this over with and be off for White's. Where are the heirs apparent—or whatever you might term them?"

Dalton scanned the ballroom. "Hmm," he said. "Don't see the trio. Perhaps they're at the refreshment table." Recalling Lady Claire's proportions, this seemed a reasonable likelihood. "Come on."

"I think you're mistaken," Chalgrove observed as he followed his lordship through the crush. "Nobody would willingly fight this mob for stale cake and lemonade."

"Oh, yes, but don't forget, there's also bread and butter." Dalton grinned over his shoulder. "Tallyho!" he whispered as he spied their quarry. Lady Sylvia was concealed from view by a bevy of beaux while she sipped the lemonade that they'd vied with one another to serve her. But the Honorable Jenny and Lady Claire stood facing in their direction.

"Where?" Chalgrove raised his quizzing glass and raked the company. All eyes, with the exception of the enthralled group around Lady Sylvia, were fixed upon him.

"There are two of them," Dalton murmured. "With Fremantle. And for God's sake, keep your voice down."

The glass moved in that direction and stopped, transfixed. Its scrutiny seemed to go on and on while the onlookers held their breath. The objects of so much attention hardly knew which way to look. Jenny, whose good humor had been quite restored since her encounter with Lord Dalton, was now beset with a mounting rage.

At last Mr. Chalgrove lowered his glass. An almost audible sigh escaped the watchers. But then the dandy whipped out a snowy handkerchief and polished the lens assiduously. He then reapplied the glass to his eye as though not really believing its previous evidence. The renewed scrutiny began at Jenny's feet, then traveled slowly up her considerable height, while an onlooker smothered a titter. Satisfied, Mr. Chalgrove then transferred his attention to Lady Claire and the glass traveled slowly from side to side. At the conclusion of this examination his seemingly nerveless fingers dropped the quizzing glass. It swung like a pendulum from its ribbon.

"Dalton, are you quite sure that these are the famous Beauties' daughters?" he inquired in a shocked and carrying tone. "Looks more like a cursed freak show to me. Come on. Let's go to White's."

There was a stunned silence. Claire's plump cheeks flamed bricky red. Jenny's turned white with fury.

"You can go to the devil, Chalgrove," Dalton growled under his breath.

"I take it you're not coming with me then?" The other smiled. "Well, suit yourself." And he turned to leave.

As he sauntered toward the doorway, Jenny hurried past him, seemingly intent upon accosting her aunt who had just entered the refreshment room. And at that very moment she somehow stumbled, sending the contents of the brimming cup of lemonade she carried down the front of Mr. Chalgrove's satin knee smalls.

The onlookers, who by that time were as synchronized as a Greek chorus, gasped even louder.

"Oh, dear, oh, dear." Jenny gazed with counterfeit consternation at Chalgrove's furious face. "How dreadfully clumsy of me. I do beg pardon, sir."

The gasps had turned to titters, and then to stifled laughter as rivulets of lemonade ran down Chalgrove's well-shaped legs to puddle by his dancing pumps. He shot the Honorable Jenny a venomous look, then whirled abruptly, and left the room. The laughter grew braver behind the dandy's back.

Lord Dalton did not join in the merriment, however. The look he bent on Jenny was grave. "I fear you've made a powerful enemy, Miss Blythe."

"Surely your mathematics are at fault, your lordship," Jenny answered, with an angelic smile. "It totals *two* enemies by my arithmetic."

Chapter Six

LADY SYLVIA, WHO had been politely attending a young gentleman's conversation, was one of the few people in his vicinity who had missed Mr. Chalgrove's "freak" remark. She had, however, witnessed Jenny's "accident" with her lemonade and was horrified that people seemed amused by the victim's soaking. So when she spied the snuffbox he'd dropped during the altercation, she snatched it up and hurried after him.

Mr. Chalgrove had a good head start and for once in his life neglected to be languid. He had, therefore, reached Almack's outer doorway when Sylvia caught sight of him. "Sir . . . Oh, sir," she called. "Could you wait a minute, please? I think you dropped this."

Chalgrove turned, his face dark with fury, prepared to vent his rage on whoever had had the temerity to accost him. But his scathing remark died aborning as he saw a vision in white hurrying toward him with an outstretched hand. Sylvia's face was sympathetic as she offered him the exquisitely enameled box. "I collect this is yours, sir, is it not? It must have rolled beneath the chair during the accident with the lemonade."

If Mr. Chalgrove had been asked an hour ago

about his attitude toward women, he would not have hesitated to admit that as a class he held them in low esteem. But there was something about this lovely innocent before him—with her look of unfeigned concern—that gave him second thoughts. He was not too far gone, however, to pick up on her words.

" 'Accident'?" he sneered.

The lovely eyes widened. "Why, of course. My cousin is not by nature clumsy, sir. But in a crush like that"—she gestured back toward the crowded rooms—"accidents will happen." She studied his soaked smalls thoughtfully, with no desire at all to titter. "I do hope the stain will come out of your breeches. Thank goodness it's lemonade, not claret. If you will instruct your valet to make a paste of honey and soft soap and then dissolve it in a strong whiskey—or I collect gin will do in a pinch—then rub it into the stain with a soft brush, it should be good as new. Oh, but tell your man he mustn't squeeze or wring the material. He should simply let it drip. And indoors, not outdoors."

Mr. Chalgrove could not quite believe his ears. And had anyone besides the doorman been within earshot, his reputation for caustic wit would have suffered to the point of total extinction. All he could find to say to this naive miss—who honestly believed he would concern himself in such a domestic matter—was a choked, "Thank you."

"I mustn't keep you standing here." Sylvia handed over the snuffbox. "This is an exquisite enamel. You would not wish to lose it, I'm sure."

Again Mr. Chalgrove's riposte was another "Thank you" as he was leveled with the sweetest smile of his experience. And when Lady Sylvia had turned away and was hurrying back toward the Assembly Rooms, he continued to watch her with a stunned look upon his face until she was completely out of sight.

An unrepentant Jenny had returned to the ballroom, where she was immediately beset by would-be partners. More than one person had felt the sting of Mr. Chalgrove's tongue and were happy to see him discomforted in turn.

At the conclusion of the boulanger she looked around the floor for Claire. She spied Lord Fremantle, making his bow to some unknown lady, and his mother, who was still gossiping with her acquaintances. Since Claire was with neither member of the family, Jenny thought it best to go in search of her.

At first glance, the cloakroom seemed deserted. But as Jenny turned away, a decorative screen caught her eye. Sure enough, her cousin was seated behind it, nibbling a chocolate daintily, determined to make it last as long as possible.

Jenny had been quick to discover that eating was her cousin's antidote for distress. "Oh, Claire," she chided. "Surely you didn't take anything that odious mushroom said to heart."

"Well he was half right, wasn't he? I, at any rate, am a freak. If you don't believe me, just ask our aunt. Or better still, my mother."

"Do you know something, Claire?" Jenny studied her cousin thoughtfully. "Self-pity does not become you. What you are is a young woman who is by no means sylphlike, but who is nonetheless extraordinarily talented and also pretty when not self-conscious. And who makes friends easily under the same condition. I cannot believe that you would react so—so—"

"Spinelessly?"

"Exactly."

"Yes, I collect I should have behaved like you and baptized him with my lemonade." Claire giggled suddenly. "Oh, Jenny, how could you? I expected all seven patronesses to converge upon you at once and march you straight out the door, never to darken these hallowed halls again."

"For an unavoidable accident?" Jenny protested, with an evil grin. "Why even Lady Jersey could not be so cruel."

"I see. An 'accident.' "

"Oh, yes, indeed. But a gloriously cathartic one. If you really had joined me in that libation to the God of Civility, I can assure you that instead of hurt feelings—" She broke off her comment as they heard voices.

"Really, Frances. You are rapidly becoming a bore."

Jenny had no difficulty in recognizing Lord Dalton's voice. She reached out a hand to stop her cousin from rising. The last thing she wanted was another confrontation with that gentleman. But then, almost immediately, she regretted the impulse. Anything would have been better than to eavesdrop upon a distasteful quarrel.

The unseen lady was obviously in the grip of a fury. "Oh, I'm boring you now, am I? You certainly were not bored when you took advantage of me and climbed into my bed."

" 'Took advantage,' Frances?" The voice was incredulous. "The only inconvenience was to me. As

I recall I had to cool my heels for quite a while waiting my turn."

There was a resounding slap, and the listening cousins winced.

"Well, I deserved that," his lordship was heard to drawl. "I hope you feel the better for it."

"You are a low-life cad, sir."

"Oh, I agree. I'm certainly not proud of cuckolding your husband. So let me suggest that you start showing him more attention. It could do wonders for your marriage."

"Oh, so it's Gerald you're concerned with, is it?" she said, with a sneer. "My husband is quite well entertained by his opera dancer, thank you. As you're quite well aware of. No, you aren't concerned with either me or him. I watched you make a cake of yourself over that whey-faced Percival brat. Why, the girl's a schoolroom miss. Half your age."

Lord Dalton found himself weary of these frequent references to his antiquity. "Half my age? I think not, Frances. I'd only give myself about a dozen years seniority to Lady Sylvia. Which is not a bad thing for a husband."

" 'Husband'?" she hissed. "You're bamming me. You wouldn't actually marry that—that—"

"Beauty? I fully intend to."

The cousins behind the screen clutched each other at this revelation and were hard-pressed not to gasp aloud.

"And I don't know why this should come as a shock to you. You knew it had to happen sooner or later."

"I knew that you were a heartless swine."

"If you say so."

"I pity the woman—or child—that does wed you. And I wish you to the devil, Dalton."

There was a swish of satin, then the cloakroom door slammed viciously.

The two cousins had turned to stone. They stared, wide-eyed at each other. Then Jenny saw Claire's eyes grow even larger, more horrified. She whirled to see Lord Dalton standing with folded arms on their side of the screen staring at them. "Something told me that we had an audience for our little scene."

Jenny, for possibly the first time in her life, was at a total loss for words. It was Lady Claire who rose to the occasion. She thrust a packet toward him. "Will you have a chocolate, sir?" she asked politely.

The buzz of conversation died abruptly when Roderick Chalgrove made his appearance at White's. He stood in the gaming-room doorway and surveyed the assembled gentlemen with cool disdain. He didn't need the sudden silence to tell him that he had been the subject of their conversation.

Indeed he was often the subject of conversation in this, the oldest and most exclusive of the gentlemen's clubs in London. Since the great George Brummell had fallen out of favor with the Regent and departed for the continent to escape his debts, Chalgrove had stepped forward to fill the gap he'd left. Of course, no one could ever hope to be the arbiter of fashion that Brummell was; still, Chalgrove had succeeded to the point that his dress and deportment were aped by White's younger members. And he and his cronies had taken over the bow-window area, once the exclusive territory of the

Brummell clique, as their particular preserve. Ordinary members, then and now, never dared to trespass.

Play had been slow throughout this evening as gambling gave precedence to gossip. First, those few members, either fresh from the country or simply shockingly uninformed, who had not heard of the Percival sisters or their daughters, had to be filled in on those details. Then Chalgrove's "freak show" comment had been passed around from the whist to the baccarat to the faro tables to be chewed on and swallowed. The majority of the membership found the remark witty. The remainder had found it rag-mannered at best, cruel at worst. Opinion was also divided as to whether the tall Percival daughter had doused Chalgrove accidentally or on purpose. The only area of agreement was that Chalgrove's humiliation was long overdue.

The members were not nearly brave enough to nudge one another or smile as the dandy made his way across the room. If all eyes tended to focus on the pristine whiteness of the evening's second pair of knee smalls, he chose to ignore the fact with a lofty disdain. Reggie York-Jones came closest to referring to the incident as he invited Chalgrove to join the play. "Didn't actually expect to see you here tonight." His impish grin died aborning, however, as Mr. Chalgrove made him the target of his famous look. "It being so late and all, I mean to say," the small man stammered.

"Late?" Chalgrove registered surprise. He swiveled in his chair to consult the mantle clock. "A mere half-past two o'clock is late?"

As a matter of fact, he was himself a bit startled by the passage of time. He had not realized that he

47

had sat in his room for quite so long before deciding to outface his fellow members, most of whom had good reason to be delighted by the Almack's incident. "I can assure you, York-Jones, that there's ample time to fleece you before daybreak."

There was something feral in his look and tone that made Lord Dalton, who had been on the point of leaving, decide to stay awhile. He gave the dandy a questioning look as he cut the cards. Chalgrove's answering smile was enigmatic.

Cards were played for lower stakes at White's than at Brook's, a club famous for deep play. Even so, when dawn brought St. James Street slowly to life, the Honorable Reginald York-Jones found himself in debt to Mr. Roderick Chalgrove for the considerable sum of one thousand pounds.

"Oh, lord," he groaned at settling-up time. "My pockets are to let right now, Chalgrove. Have to give you my vowel, I'm afraid."

"Sorry, Reggie. I don't think I can accept it."

The other players paused in the act of polishing off the dregs of the brandy to stare at Chalgrove.

"Now see here," York-Jones sputtered. "I'm good for your blasted thousand pounds. Never welched on a wager in my life. It's just that my quarterly allowance ain't due for two weeks yet."

Dalton looked from one to the other. York-Jones's face was rapidly reddening at the insult. Chalgrove was counting his winnings, quite unconcerned by the shocked stares of the other players.

"I can let you have the blunt, Reggie," Dalton said. "That is," he added dryly, "if Chalgrove here will hold *my* vowel till the bank opens."

"Oh, that won't be necessary." Mr. Chalgrove waved away the suggestion. "There seems to be some misunderstanding. I know that Reggie's good for it. I just don't happen to want his money. I've a much better way for him to discharge his debt."

The smile he bent upon the Honorable Reginald did little to alleviate that young gentleman's discomfort.

Chapter Seven

As the hour for morning calls drew near, Lady Fremantle grew more and more agitated. "No one will come," she moaned for the thousandth time. "We're ruined. You'll see." The words were directed at the Honorable Jenny.

Since their departure from Almack's the evening before, her ladyship had harped on this one theme. They had barely settled themselves in the crested carriage when she had burst into noisy tears. "You've ruined us," she had wailed at Jenny. "Oh, how could you? Don't you know that Mr. Chalgrove can make or break us with Society?"

"No, ma'am, I didn't know. The fact certainly doesn't speak well for Society, does it?"

"Don't give me any more examples of your impertinence," her ladyship had stormed. "If you wished to ruin your own chances—well, that's one thing. But to ruin your cousins' as well—that's unforgivable!"

"Now, now, Mama," Fremantle had said soothingly. "I collect you're blowing the incident out of all proportion. I grant you that Mr. Chalgrove is something of an ape-leader. But even he must know that accidents will happen."

" 'Accidents'!" Her ladyship was unmollified.

"Accidents," her stepson repeated firmly. "And even if Mr. Chalgrove is so small-minded as to think otherwise, I'm convinced it will not be the general opinion. I think the evening went very well, actually. In fact, I can safely say that my cousins' debut into society was a success."

Her ladyship sniffed. But the tears had ceased to flow. "Lord Dalton did stand up twice with Sylvia, did he not? And Lady Jersey herself whispered to me that his lordship appeared quite taken. And certainly his consequence is at least the equal of Mr. Chalgrove's. Or larger. Most definitely, larger. For if their fortunes are about the same—well, there's the title to be considered." She was cheered for just a moment, but then as the carriage turned into Grosvenor Square, she succumbed to the dismals once again. "Still, they're thick as thieves. So if Mr. Chalgrove chooses to cut us, I'm certain that Lord Dalton will follow his lead."

Good, was Jenny's private thought. But she was already too much in her aunt's disfavor to dare speak it aloud.

If she had hoped that the dawn of a new day would bring Lady Fremantle a new perspective, Jenny was doomed to disappointment. She bit her lip to keep from saying, For heaven's sake, do sit still, as her aunt crossed the drawing room for the third time in so many minutes to stare out the window at the street below. "No one is coming," she sighed. "What did I tell you?"

"Well, at least Lord Dalton's sure to come." Claire looked up from the tambouring she was engaged in to speak soothingly.

Her well-meant remark brought on a fresh outburst. "What a goosish thing to say. How can you,

51

of all people, possibly hope to know what Lord Dalton would do?"

Claire reddened as Jenny shot her a warning look. "I d-don't, of course. It's just that you did say he stood up with Sylvia twice. And so I thought—"

"You thought!" her aunt replied witheringly.

Sylvia, who had been reading, or at least holding a copy of *La Belle Assemblee* upon her lap, closed it to try to act as peacemaker. "I cannot speak for Lord Dalton, either," she said mildly. "But I'm certain that your friends will call on us, Aunt. I do believe you've underestimated your own consequence in dwelling upon Mr. Chalgrove's. Why, several of the young gentlemen told me last night that their fathers had expressly asked them to meet us, merely because they have such fond memories of you and your sisters."

"That is true." Lady Fremantle preened herself a bit. "The Percivals still count for something in our generation. But still"—she quickly reverted to her former gloom—"the young men of today aren't like their fathers. They don't think for themselves. Mark my words, it will only take one word from that odious Mr. Chalgrove to ruin us."

If this was so, it soon became obvious that Mr. Chalgrove had not yet delivered that fatal word. For shortly after Lady Fremantle's prophetic utterance, a steady stream of young gentlemen came calling. Lady Sylvia was the magnet that drew them, as Lord Dalton discovered to his chagrin when he, too, entered the withdrawing room.

Although it was almost three o'clock he had struggled from his bed only a short while earlier. His eyes were bloodshot. He suffered from the headache. Calling on a green young girl, no matter how beautiful, was the last thing on earth he wished to do. To say the least, his mood was far from sunny. Nor did it brighten when he stood in the doorway and observed the gaggle of swains clustered around Lady Sylvia. It suffered a total eclipse when he noted that the only available place to sit was on a sofa next to the Honorable Jenny Blythe. Lady Claire, who was diligently tambouring, somewhat removed from the crush around her cousin, looked alarmed when he did so.

"Well, you certainly look like a dire warning against dissipation," was Jenny's word of greeting. "Have a late evening, did you?"

"You do delight in going for the jugular, don't you, Miss Blythe?"

"Not at all. In fact, I've taken your preachment very much to heart. What I really wished to say is that you look like the very devil. I was using restraint, you see."

" 'Restraint'? I doubt you know the meaning of the word. Did you, for instance, restrain yourself from telling Lady Sylvia of the cloakroom conversation you overheard?"

"Now who's dealing in plain speaking? To be equally as blunt, I'm hoping that won't be necessary, Lord Dalton."

"Oh? And why not, if I dare ask."

"My hope is that in the cold light of day you'll realize yourself how unsuitable you are for my young cousin. And then I won't be obliged to repeat what I overheard."

"Blackmail, Miss Blythe?"

"If you so choose to label it."

"I see no need to wrap your tactics in clean linen. I also refuse to be victimized. Say anything you wish—to anyone you wish—Miss Blythe. Eavesdropping is a waste of time otherwise, is it not?"

"I was certainly not eavesdropping," she said, bristling. "I'll have you know that my cousin and I were already in the cloakroom before you and your—whatever—staged your little scene."

"Concealed behind a screen. That's surely odd behavior."

"Where else should we tie our garters?"

"You could have coughed, you know."

"We could do no such thing. You and your *friend* were well into your row before you ever entered." She tried to modify her heated tone as her aunt frowned in their direction. "Isn't your proper fifteen minutes up?" she whispered pointedly.

"That won't work, Miss Blythe. I'll not leave till I speak to your cousin." He rose to his feet. "I think I can now beat my way through the throng. Good day, Miss Blythe."

"I was hoping you'd be reasonable," she sighed. "You should know, Lord Dalton, that I intend to do everything in my power to throw a rub in your way."

"And you should know, Miss Blythe, that you are sadly overmatched."

He'd never spoken a truer word, Jenny thought glumly as she watched him edge the would-be suitors away from Sylvia. Jenny was too far away to hear what was being said, although she strained her ears to do so. She wondered what Dalton might be like when he exerted himself to please, a condition she would never experience firsthand, she realized.

She was overmatched all right. He was rich, handsome— Here Jenny firmly put a stop to the catalog of Dalton's assets and dwelled on the one important fact. He was bound to be a total disaster as a husband. Especially for someone as seemingly gentle and sensitive as her cousin Sylvia. And it was all very well to announce that she planned to put a rub in his way, but how? Sylvia might or might not be put off by an account of the cloakroom scene. That men had mistresses was a fact of life. How Dalton had got rid of his would probably lose a great deal in the telling. You really needed to be there to appreciate the nastiness.

Well, one ploy would be to see to it that Sylvia was not left alone with his disagreeable lordship. And it was futile to expect any help from her aunt in achieving this end. Jenny had rejected the idea of telling Lady Fremantle about the cloakroom incident. She would simply be ecstatic over Dalton's declared intentions, never mind the reflection upon his character. She was already in transports over the mere possibility of such a match and was certain to throw the two together as much as possible. No, if there was to be any chaperoning done, she, Jenny, would have to do it. And from the way Dalton was smiling down at Sylvia, he was on the point of suggesting some kind of tête-à-tête. She had best move fast.

"Oh, Mr. West," she called in a carrying voice to one of the young gentlemen who had been supplanted by Lord Dalton. "My cousins and I plan to spend the next several days seeing the sights of London. We particularly long to view the Elgin Marbles. Can you suggest a time when we might best avoid the crush?"

Mr. West could do better than that. He could personally escort the ladies to Burlington House tomorrow.

"Claire? Sylvia? Would that suit?" Jenny studiously ignored the glare that Lady Fremantle sent her way. "Oh, good, then. That's settled."

There was a sudden competition among the other gentlemen present to offer themselves as guides to the metropolis. Jenny, who had spent hours pouring over the guidebook she had purchased for five shillings, began to tick off the places that the three of them most longed to see. If the young gentlemen were somewhat daunted by the prospect of having to drag along her cousins in order to spend time with Lady Sylvia, they were too well-bred to show it. Perhaps it was the formidable prospect of Lord Dalton as a rival that made them eager to pay any price for a few hours spent in the company of the nonpareil. Jenny was swamped with eager volunteers. She made quick arrangements for visits to Westminster Abbey, St. Paul's, the Tower, the Guildhall, the British Museum.

"Well, that should certainly keep us occupied for a while." She smiled politely, rejecting one gentleman's suggestion that they really should visit the museum more than once. "I do believe I've scheduled all the free time we'll have available for weeks now."

"You most certainly have," her aunt replied icily.

"And a deadly boring job you've made of it." Lord Dalton forced a smile—while eyeing her with a look that left no doubt he knew what she was up to. "As an antidote to all those educational excursions, may I suggest a spectacle at Astley's Amphitheatre? I shall be pleased to take you three ladies there."

"Oh, I don't think so." Jenny's smile was just as

false. "It's kind of your lordship to concern yourself, but a spectacle seems so—childish."

" 'Childish'!" Lady Fremantle sputtered. "It is no such thing. Why, *everybody* goes there. Sylvia, you are sure to like it above all things. My nieces will be delighted to accept your kind invitation, Lord Dalton."

"Good. That's settled then." He rose to go, favoring Lady Sylvia with a charming smile, then bowing slightly to Jenny, a mocking gleam in his narrowed eyes.

Chapter Eight

"WELL, WE CERTAINLY did not lack for callers," Jenny said brightly when the final visitor had gone. "It appears that your worries were unfounded, aunt. Mr. Chalgrove has not sent us to Coventry. Indeed, I think things went very well."

" 'Well'!" Her ladyship unleashed the wrath that had been building within her breast for the past hour or more. " 'Well,' you say. Of all the brassfaced, forward exhibitions! How dare you monopolize all of your cousin's time that way? I'm sure that Sylvia is capable of making her own plans. And I'm also certain that Lord Dalton—quite the biggest catch in London, as if you didn't know—was on the point of asking if he might drive her in the park when you cut him off with your silly arrangements."

"Well, he did make it onto our list," Jenny replied mildly.

"No thanks to you! And you've given him no opportunity to spend time alone with Sylvia. Which was obviously his only reason for coming here. You should have allowed *her* to decide."

"But I don't mind in the least," Sylvia interposed. "Indeed, I think Jenny's plans are famous. I'd much rather that we all went places together than ride alone with Lord Dalton. I'm sure I'd never think of a thing to say to him."

"You wouldn't need to," Lady Fremantle snapped. "He has enough address for both of you. And you'd do well, miss, to recall just why you're here. Your objective is to get a husband, not visit every fusty place listed in that odious guidebook. And if Lord Dalton makes any alternative suggestions to the regimen your cousin has entangled you in, you are to accept his invitations. Do you understand? Not wish to ride with Lord Dalton indeed! What your mother would have to say to such foolishness I cannot imagine. But I can assure you that when we sisters made our come-outs we kept our eyes wide open—to recognize the best chances when we saw them."

"I'm sure that you did, Aunt Lydia."

There was no insolence in Sylvia's tone, but there was something about it that caused Jenny to stare at her cousin curiously. There was no time to search for nuances, however, for Lady Fremantle's wrath descended once again upon her head.

"I can only conclude, miss, that you are jealous of your cousin's popularity since you chose to interfere with her opportunities in this flagrant manner. In the future you are to make no more arrangements without first discussing them with me."

At this point Claire, who had endured as much misery as she could bear for one afternoon, mumbled a quick "Pray excuse me," and fled before her aunt could direct any part of the scold her way. Her mind was upon the lovely box of chocolates hidden in her room. She felt that she had certainly earned one of the delicious confections. Or two, perhaps. She was hurrying toward her bedchamber when her attention was caught by the sound of someone playing the pianoforte very skillfully.

Claire loved music above all things. The chocolates could wait. She followed the sound to its source. Her stepcousin was seated at the instrument in the smaller gold withdrawing room playing Mozart with half-closed eyes. He appeared, in fact, to have been transported to some other sphere. It was some moments before he sensed Claire's presence in the doorway and stopped abruptly.

"Oh, I do beg pardon, Cousin Claire. I'd no idea that you were standing there. Did you wish to see me?"

"Oh, no," she breathed, then looked embarrassed. "What I mean to say is, please don't stop. I heard you playing. And it's so beautiful. I'd no idea you played at all, Cousin James, let alone so marvelously. Please, do go on. Mozart is my particular favorite."

He flushed with pleasure and then continued. She left her position by the door to stand where she could watch his fingers on the keyboard. When the last note had faded away, she stood enthralled; her eyes were misty.

"Oh, thank you," she breathed. "That was lovely. I play that piece myself, but not half so well."

He laughed dismissively. "Now you're flattering me, cousin. I'm the merest amateur."

"Oh, no, you are not," she replied earnestly. "That is to say, of course you are in the sense that you don't perform for money. But if you were not Lord Fremantle"—her gaze took in the elegant room as if to suggest all that his title implied—"you could easily play professionally."

"Not really," he replied candidly. "Oh, I'd like

to think I could, with assiduous practice, acquire the necessary skill. But the very thought of facing a hall full of people would give me the horrors."

She nodded sympathetically. "I know exactly what you mean. My mother was always pushing me to perform for her friends. But she finally gave it up. My fingers would turn to sticks from terror, and my throat would tighten till I could merely squeak. But it's a great pity that you should suffer in the same way. For you should be heard. You have the gift of taking a person right out of herself with your playing. It's easy to forget—everything—while listening. You should never stop." She smiled.

He picked up on her wistfulness. "Has the day been trying then? Jackson tells me that the house was fairly awash with callers. After my stepmother's dire predictions, I thought everyone would be in raptures."

"Well, Aunt Lydia was pleased by the number of gentlemen who visited. All to see Sylvia, of course."

Lord Fremantle gave her a sharp look, but there was no sign of resentment on her countenance. She appeared merely to accept this as fact.

"But then she turned positively livid at Jenny's behavior." Claire went on to tell him how her cousin had recruited Sylvia's suitors to serve as guides for all three of them. "It was obvious that Aunt Lydia longed to throttle her, but could think of no graceful way to put a stop to her maneuvers."

"But I don't really understand what was so terrible. My cousin may have been a trifle forward, but surely not so forward as to give offense."

"Well, Aunt Lydia accused her of using Sylvia's popularity to secure escorts for herself and me. But that wasn't it at all. Oh, Jenny did joke earlier about using Sylvia for a Judas goat to attract gentlemen. But it was only a joke."

"And a poor one, I'd say." Fremantle frowned.

"The truth is, Jenny was trying to put off Lord Dalton. To block him from a serious pursuit of Sylvia."

"I don't understand. Does Cousin Jenny want Dalton for herself? I remember she did make that remark at Almack's about choosing him, but I thought she was merely funning."

"Oh, she was. In truth, she doesn't like him above half. That's it, you see. She knows he's not at all suitable for Sylvia. Whereas Aunt Lydia is quite determined to throw her at his head."

"I'm surprised to hear myself say so"—Fremantle smiled crookedly—"but I'm in complete agreement with my stepmama. Dalton is, and has been for donkey's years, the matrimonial prize of London. I do not approve of throwing Sylvia at his head, of course. That's bound to disgust him, I should think. Far too many mamas have tried that already. Perhaps Mama should be grateful to Jenny for making Sylvia appear not quite so desperate."

"Is Lord Dalton so very rich, then?" Claire asked curiously.

"A regular nabob."

"Well, I still don't think he's right for Sylvia." She wrinkled her nose in distaste.

"Why ever not? Except for a disparity in years—Dalton's my age. We were in school together, actually, though in different sets, of course. But as I was saying, except for an age difference, I don't see why they shouldn't suit."

"Oh, I don't object to that at all. I think Sylvia might actually like someone a bit older. She's rather biddable. At least for the most part. I will say she has her own ideas on certain things, though. She vetoed the gown our aunt had chosen for Jenny's come-out. She said it was entirely unsuitable for her type. And neither Aunt Lydia nor that odious modiste could budge her."

Fremantle's lips twitched. "That does show remarkable resolution. But I doubt that Dalton would try to run over her roughshod. I must say I'm surprised, Cousin Claire, by your aversion to the man. Ever since I've known him, Dalton has been everyone's beau ideal. Just what is it you object to?"

The question was a poser. Even if the cloakroom incident were not entirely too delicate to relate to a member of the opposite sex, Jenny had sworn her to secrecy. "It's just that I've heard that Lord Dalton is a man of poor character," she offered rather lamely.

He looked amazed. "You heard that? Well, it's news to me. Someone must have been jealous to blacken his name like that. If I were you, I'd discount it as slander. I can assure you, he's entirely honorable."

"Even in his dealings with women?" So much then for propriety.

Fremantle looked uncomfortable. "I don't pretend to keep abreast of such. But I don't doubt that he has—has had throughout the years—certain liaisons. But you mustn't make too much of this. While I can't say I approve of . . . certain conduct,

I fear that if you eliminate every suitor who has had dalliances, the marriage rate would decline shockingly.

"No, really, cousin, I think you refine too much on malicious gossip. I will vouch for Dalton. If he should become enamored of our cousin Sylvia, there's no reason to be otherwise than pleased. Frankly, I'm more concerned that she will get her hopes dashed. It has happened to more than one young Beauty, I understand."

"Well, perhaps you're right," Claire said doubtfully. "At any rate, that's quite enough about Lord Dalton. Would you please play something else? There's still a bit of time before we need dress for dinner."

He was more than willing to oblige. She stood, enthralled, while he played a long medley of Irish airs. "Oh, that was marvelous," she breathed when he'd finished.

"As much as you love music, you must take advantage of your visit and hear some of the truly great performers. Do you like opera, Cousin Claire?"

"I've never been."

"You haven't?" He was amazed. "Well, we must rectify that. I'll speak to my stepmama. We'll make up a party as soon as possible."

"Oh, I'd like that above all things." Her eyes shone with pleasure.

"It's settled then. Now I expect we had better dress for dinner. If her ladyship is up in the boughs already, it would never do to upset her further by being late."

Claire hurried to her room, her thoughts filled with the coming treat. For the first time she was actually looking forward to an event in London. She dressed for dinner with unusual care. And it was only as she closed her bedchamber door behind her that she realized she'd forgotten all about her chocolates.

Chapter Nine

THE NEXT SEVERAL days were taken up with a flurry of activities. Besides the outings Jenny had arranged, the cousins were deluged with invitations. But all this was prelude. Lady Fremantle was determined that her own ball should be the most talked of party of the Season.

She had a finger in every pie of preparation. Mrs. O'Hara had threatened to quit if her ladyship changed the menu one more time. The orchestra leader had been driven to exclaim that he was quite capable of choosing suitable music without her help. Had the Prince Regent ever complained? The butler informed her stiffly that there was no need to order more wine; their own cellar was more than adequate for the occasion. The footmen threatened to walk out in a body if her ladyship issued one more order only to countermand it an hour later.

But no aspect had received greater attention than the guest list. Every eligible male in town had been asked. Lady Fremantle had even scoured the country estates for possible suitors. When Jenny, who along with her cousins had been addressing cards till her hand ached, wondered at this, the curt answer was, "I think you and Claire might be most comfortable with some country squire."

"Well, you're probably right." Jenny refused to be offended. "A regular bumpkin would be preferable to this bit of town bronze." She wrinkled her nose with distaste at the next name on her list. "Why on earth are you inviting Mr. Chalgrove?"

"Everybody invites Mr. Chalgrove. His presence assures a function's success. He seldom accepts, of course. And after what you did, he certainly won't accept our invitation." The memory still rankled.

"Why ask him then?"

"Didn't I just explain?" Lady Fremantle's nerves were reaching the raw stage. "Everyone invites Mr. Chalgrove."

"Oh, I see." The three young ladies exchanged looks across the library table and tried hard to keep from smiling.

No amount of planning could control the weather. The day began with a downpour that later moderated but refused to go away. An awning was erected from the portico to the street, but Lady Fremantle was convinced that no one would show up to use it.

She was wrong, of course, a circumstance that surprised no one but her. By then her nieces had grown accustomed to the fact that she took the gloomiest view of all occasions. Indeed, it seemed that no one had disregarded her invitation. The number of guests soon swelled into a veritable crush, that uncomfortable state of affairs every hostess longs for.

The first indication that Lady Fremantle's ball was to be an unqualified success was the arrival of Lord Dalton, more elegant even than usual in white satin knee breeches and a white waistcoat, topped off by a black coat with very long tails.

While not quite as elusive as Mr. Chalgrove, he

was known to avoid those gatherings where he was certain to be bored. But not only had he accepted the invitation to Fremantle House, he was among the earlier arrivals. Lord Dalton, as his former tutors could have testified, was not backward. He wanted no repetition of the Almack's fiasco. This time he not only secured the first dance with Sylvia, he engaged her for his supper partner as well.

Then, when Mr. Chalgrove arrived only minutes later, Lady Fremantle was beside herself. She was trying to decide whether to apologize for her niece's clumsiness at Almack's or to pretend it had never happened, when Mr. Chalgrove quickly put a period to her effusive greeting. With a curt nod to Fremantle, who along with his stepmama was receiving guests, he passed on into the ballroom. Mr. Chalgrove was closely trailed by the Honorable Reginald York-Jones who tried, quite unsuccessfully, to ape his mentor's air of world-weariness.

Unlike Dalton, Mr. Chalgrove seemed content merely to watch the dancing. He positioned himself near the doorway and eyed proceedings through his quizzing glass. The glass seemed to rest overly long upon Lady Sylvia, who was dancing a cotillion with Lord Dalton. Dressed in pale blue, she had never looked more lovely. When he at last forced his gaze away, he had no trouble at all locating the Honorable Jenny Blythe. She had no need to resort to the ostrich plumes that topped the coiffures of so many of the ladies present in order to stand out above the crowd. Even Mr. Chalgrove had to acknowledge that she looked quite elegant. The British net she wore over rose satin effectively set off her dark hair and sparkling eyes.

"Now." As the cotillion ended, Chalgrove gave

the diminutive gentleman beside him the briefest of nods.

"Now? Right, then. Seems a deuced easy way to cancel a—" He caught Chalgrove's frown and broke off what he was about to say. "See you a bit later."

Mr. York-Jones began to elbow his way through the crush—no easy matter for a gentleman his size—to eventually wind up where Jenny had found a seat in one of the rout chairs that ringed the wall. "Will you grant me the honor of this dance, Miss Blythe?"

Jenny interrupted a conversation with the young woman beside her to turn and gaze into the eyes of a small, personable young man. He seemed to be having a great deal of difficulty containing his mirth. She immediately saw the joke and laughed back at the irrepressible pixie. "You are aware then that the next dance is a waltz?"

"Oh, yes, indeed."

"Then if you're game, I am."

She stood, feeling rather like a spyglass unfolding, and took the arm he proffered.

When they were positioned on the dance floor and he'd clasped her waist and hand, his eyes were on an exact level with her décolletage. A thought struck her. "You came with Mr. Chalgrove, did you not?"

The music cut off his reply, but no confirmation was needed. She'd caught a glimpse of Mr. Chalgrove leveling his glass their way. Lord Dalton stood frowning there beside him.

A miniature whirlwind seemed to have sprung up for the purpose of sweeping her into the dance. Jenny soon discovered that her partner possessed extraordinary skill, despite—or perhaps because of—his size. And she had taught too many little brothers and sisters how to waltz to be disconcerted by a partner whom she dwarfed. As they circled the ballroom, weaving skillfully in and out of the mass of spinning couples, Mr. York-Jones twinkled up at her, and she laughed back. All eyes appeared fixed upon them. Jenny was enjoying herself immensely.

"If you'd hoped to make her look ridiculous, I don't think it's working," Dalton remarked dryly to his crony. He had just admitted, grudgingly, to himself that the tall, willowy waltzer looked magnificent.

The other shrugged. "Well, it was worth a try. It's always difficult to give a setdown to a female. You never have the slightest notion of how the creatures will react."

"Aren't you being a bit petty, old fellow?"

"Undoubtedly. But one must find amusement in these tiresome gatherings any way one can."

"Well, you could always dance."

"Do you know, that odd notion had just occurred to me. Do excuse me, will you, Dalton."

With an exaggerated bow, Chalgrove left his station by the wall and worked his way around the perimeter of the ballroom. Dalton's face betrayed none of his uneasiness as the dandy approached Lady Sylvia, who was fanning herself after the exertions of the waltz. But he did not miss the shy smile she gave Mr. Chalgrove as he led her into the dance.

Lady Fremantle was none too pleased. She had been quite content to have her stepson engage Claire's hand for the initial dance. He was a conscientious young man and could be counted upon to do his duty by his cousins. But standing up with Lady Claire a second time went well beyond the call of duty. Particularly since it was no secret that Lord Fremantle loathed dancing. It was bound to cause a bit of tittle-tattle. Her ladyship decided to nip it in the bud.

Her eyes scanned the gentlemen scattered here and there about the ballroom who were unpartnered. They settled on a callow, spotted youth. She bore down upon him with a determined smile and ushered him across the ballroom, murmuring instructions in his ear as she did so.

"My dear James." She accosted her stepson just as he and Claire were moving toward the dance floor. "I cannot allow you to monopolize your cousin in this fashion. Mr. Brett has been longing for a dance." Her smile seemed permanently etched. "Lady Claire, may I present the Honorable Wesley Brett? Hurry, m'dears, before the sets are all made up. Now come along, James. You mustn't shirk your hostly duties." He trailed obediently behind her.

Two of her ladyship's bosom bows had watched the incident with interest. They gave each other knowing looks and began to whisper behind their fans.

Miss Blythe and Mr. York-Jones were well pleased with each other. They both shared a lively sense of the absurd, as they discovered when recovering from their spirited waltz. They found two empty chairs near the orchestra and sipped fruit punch thirstily while York-Jones kept Jenny in stitches with his comments about this or that person on the floor. As he spied Jenny's next partner bearing down upon them, he quickly asked to take her in to supper.

"I'd be delighted." She smiled down at him. "That is, if you are following your own inclinations and not Mr. Chalgrove's orders."

"Both, actually."

"Oh, well." She shrugged. "If a mere disparity in size can give that gentleman amusement, who am I to begrudge him his entertainment? It all seems rather odd, though. But then I expect he is. Odd, I mean."

"Oh, no, not really." York-Jones was ready to leap to the defense of one of his idols, but he was not given the opportunity. Jenny's next partner had arrived and was offering his arm.

If he'd any plans to resume his advocacy at supper, they were thwarted, for Miss Blythe seemed determined to take refreshments with her cousins. She had seized upon Lady Claire and the spotty youth who had dutifully asked to be her supper partner, and the four had joined the crowd making its way to the supper room together. Lord Dalton did not look best pleased when he reappeared with Lady Sylvia's supper plate to find Miss Blythe seated by his vacant chair. His spirits felt no lift when Mr. Chalgrove joined their group a bit later. "You still here?" was his less-than-cordial greeting.

"Can't tear myself away, as you see." Uninvited, he insinuated a chair between Lady Sylvia and York-Jones. "And since you seem the most scintillating group among all this scintillating company—well, even at the peril of my knee smalls"—he gazed speculatively toward Jenny—"I was determined to join you."

"Oh, I think you're at a safe enough distance, sir." There was a tinge of regret in Jenny's tone.

"I am relieved." He took a sip of champagne, his only supper. "But don't let me interrupt the merriment. Far be it from me to cast a pall. What were you speaking of when I so rudely interrupted?"

"Mr. York-Jones was telling us about Lord Alvanley." Sylvia spoke in a conspiratorial voice, directing his attention toward a group of the more mature guests gathered around their hostess. "He has had us in stitches."

"Oh?" Chalgrove stifled a yawn. "And which oft-told tale was it? The apricot tart? Really, Reggie, must you bore the ladies?"

"They may be 'oft-told' in your circles," Sylvia retorted, "but I can assure you, we were not the least bit bored. Quite the contrary, in fact. He was telling us that Lord Alvanley had a friend who hated staying in the country because the quiet got on his nerves. So Alvanley hired a hackney coach to drive underneath the friend's window all night long." She laughed—and looked enchanting as she did so.

"You're right, of course. That is a wonderful story. I stand corrected," Chalgrove said humbly. Lord Dalton gave him a suspicious look.

"Yes," York-Jones chimed in. "And I was just about to add that he had the boots call out the time and the weather on the hour." The others, excluding Mr. Chalgrove, joined his laughter.

That gentleman was surveying the assembled guests thoughtfully, too absorbed even to employ his quizzing glass. "Lady Fremantle has achieved a sort of social miracle," he observed dryly. "Why, there are husbands and wives here together who I

73

daresay haven't spoken in ages—some of whom no longer make a pretense of living together. It certainly speaks volumes for her ladyship's reputation as a hostess.

"No, let me amend that, somewhat," he mused on. "I suspect this in a sense a reunion for all those of a certain age. A harking back, as it were, to the glory days. For as our elders are all too fond of telling us, there was never a Season like the one in 1797 when the famous Percival sisters made their entrée into Society. Oh, by the by, Lady Claire, I seem to have missed your father in the crush. Surely he's here somewhere? After all, he was one of the fortunate foursome who managed to capture a Percival prize. I know he wouldn't miss this for the world."

There was a long, uncomfortable pause. Lord Dalton's face was granite. Mr. York-Jones seemed not to know which way to look. Lady Claire had blushed an unbecoming red. She was forced to swallow before she could answer. "My father is abroad, sir."

"Indeed?" Mr. Chalgrove's eyebrows rose. "Was he called away suddenly then? I could have sworn I saw him in Pall Mall only yesterday. But then, of course, I may have been mistaken. For," he added slyly, "I understand that he rarely wanders far from Russel Street these days."

"I think you're confusing my father with someone else, sir." Claire appeared close to tears. "His direction is Berkeley Square."

Jenny was trying, unsuccessfully, to think of a way to divert the conversation when Sylvia was suddenly stricken. She slumped in her chair, moaned pathetically, and weakly fanned herself.

74

All eyes turned toward her. "Are you all right?" Jenny asked anxiously.

Sylvia's quivering smile was brave. "I'm just feeling a bit faint, that's all."

The gentlemen were all consternation, offering to fetch glasses of water and/or brandy; sal volatile and/or burned feathers; Lady Fremantle and/or her abigail.

"Thank you so very much." Sylvia's voice was weak. "But that won't be at all necessary. If I lie down a few moments, I'm sure to be myself again. These little—upsets—never last long. Cousin Claire, forgive my selfishness in dragging you away. But would you mind very much coming with me? You always seem to know exactly how to rub my temples when I have these little spells."

It was difficult to say whether Lady Claire looked more mystified or relieved as she rose to accompany her cousin. Lady Sylvia's expression was much easier to decipher. The look she bent on Mr. Chalgrove was censorious in the extreme.

Chapter Ten

Mr. Roderick Chalgrove committed a social solecism by calling at Fremantle House the following morning. When he asked to see Lady Sylvia, the butler, at his most starchy, was in the very act of telling him that her ladyship was not in the habit of receiving guests on the day following an all-night ball, when Sylvia herself came down the stairs and overheard. "Oh, Jackson, I will see Mr. Chalgrove," she called. Making no attempt to hide his disapproval, the majordomo opened the front door wide.

Lady Sylvia ushered Mr. Chalgrove into the smallest of her aunt's three withdrawing rooms and ordered tea. Jackson served them himself, exuding disapproval. After the butler had left them, Chalgrove smiled ruefully. "I'm certainly in your butler's black book. But I had to see how you were feeling after your fit of the vapors last night."

Mr. Chalgrove had spoken the simple truth. After he had finally gone to bed he had tossed and turned for the little that remained of the night, going over and over the scene that had led up to Sylvia's seizure. Every time he began to drift toward sleep, her parting look came back to haunt him and force him wide awake once more.

"Did I understand you right, Lady Sylvia? You're prone to frequent fainting spells?"

Sylvia looked embarrassed. "Why, no. As a matter of fact, I've never swooned in my life. It was simply the only way I could think of to get you to hush."

"Indeed?" He was, for an instant, his usual top-lofty self. "Was I that boring?"

Her look was impatient. "You know perfectly well what I'm referring to, Mr. Chalgrove. You were upsetting my cousin Claire dreadfully, referring to her father in that manner. My cousin Jenny says you did it deliberately to hurt her. But I'll not believe that."

Now it was his turn to feel uncomfortable. "I merely spoke the truth," he said defensively. "I did see her father in Pall Mall."

"Then you should have stopped to think before you said so."

There was a long pause. The tea tray lay untouched between them. Mr. Chalgrove came close to squirming before her reproachful gaze. He caught himself wondering whether his mother, if she had lived beyond his birth, might have acted in just this way. He felt five years old of a sudden.

Then, remembering who he was, Mr. Chalgrove rallied. But an icy setdown, intended to put this schoolroom miss in her proper place, died on his lips. For some hidden reason he couldn't search for at the moment, he found her large, trusting eyes devastating. He tried to bluff.

"Lady Sylvia, I'm noted for my scorching tongue. They say I can level strong men with a single sentence. Indeed I've actually been called out on two occasions for rather witty remarks at which certain

77

gentlemen took umbrage. But for the life of me, I don't see what was so terrible about mentioning I'd seen your cousin's father. If Lord Hazlett chose to dodge his sister-in-law's ball, I for one would hardly blame him."

"My cousin Claire would. As you should have realized."

"I should? Why in heaven's name should I have that sort of insight?"

"Oh, come now. You, like everyone else in town, have been aware of all the foolish talk about the famous Percival sisters. And how everyone expected their daughters to repeat their triumph. Don't tell me you have not."

It was apparent to Mr. Chalgrove that no one had repeated his freak show remark to her. His relief surprised him. "Why, yes. I've heard a bit of talk," he admitted cautiously.

"Well, the whole idea is patently absurd." Sylvia picked up the teapot and poured. He watched apprehensively as the liquid splashed with her indignation. "We are different people entirely. My cousin Jenny, for example, looks nothing like the Percivals. I happen to think she looks much, much better." Her look was challenging as she thrust a porcelain cup toward him. "She's tall and striking. She makes the Percivals look ... insipid. And as for my cousin Claire—well, you must see that her weight could be the subject of cruel jests. Her mother—whom I consider a *monster* even if she is my aunt—has made no secret of the fact that her daughter is an embarrassment. She would not even come to London for Claire's come-out. Now you have made it appear that her father feels the same. It was a cruel, even if unintentional, thing to do. I repeat, sir, you should have stopped to think."

"I can only say, Lady Claire, that I'm sorry." Chalgrove spoke softly. He was amazed to realize his words were true. They sat in silence, sipping their tea for a moment. Then he was overcome by curiosity.

"But what about you, Lady Sylvia? You've pointed out that your cousins don't measure up to the Percival standard. That leaves only you to uphold the family tradition, as it were. Well, it's obvious that you more than make up for any—err—variations—in the other two. I studied the famous Romney portrait carefully last night. And in my opinion you far outshine your mother and your aunts. So I'd say the Percival legend lives on."

If such a lovely face could ever contrive to look fierce, Lady Sylvia's achieved it. Mr. Chalgrove was startled out of his last vestige of aplomb as he stared at her.

"I, sir, am *not* a Percival." She tossed her head defiantly. "Nor have I any desire to be one. I, Mr. Chalgrove, am Lady Sylvia *Kinnard.*"

Lord Dalton arrived at Grosvenor Square just as Jackson was ushering Mr. Chalgrove out the door. His lordship drew his watch from his pocket and looked pointedly at it. "For a high stickler in the world of fashion, aren't you a bit previous, Chalgrove?"

"Mine wasn't a social call," was the other's enigmatic answer.

"Can't tell you how relieved I am to hear that. It would be a pity if you and I turned out to be rivals for the same lady's hand."

79

"Oh? And just which of the young ladies would that be, Dalton?"

"After your tasteless remark at Almack's, that doesn't even deserve an answer."

"Touché! But the idea of you pursuing *any* female with an eye toward matrimony is staggering."

"The time comes for us all sooner or later. Even you are bound to succumb."

"Oh, no. I'm immune to that particular disease." The dandy tilted his high-crowned hat at a rakish angle.

"Well, let's hope the immunity doesn't lose its effect in the near future. It could prove awkward."

"Are you threatening me, Dalton?"

"What an absurd notion. I'm just pointing out that this is not the time for you to abandon your role of London's leading misogynist. Good day, Chalgrove."

The gentlemen bowed to each other politely. Both frowned as they went their separate ways.

Lord Dalton's intent was to engage Lady Sylvia for a drive in the park later that afternoon. Since he did not plan to linger any longer than it took to issue an invitation, he left his rig in the street with his tiger in charge. Right after the front door had closed behind his lordship, Jenny, trailed by one of Lady Fremantle's maids, returned from a ribbon-buying excursion. She stopped short to admire the high-perch phaeton. Lord Dalton emerged a few moments later to find that his equipage had disappeared.

He was on the portico—leaning against a Corinthian column with fire in his eyes—when his rig rounded the corner. His tiger, dressed in scarlet livery resplendent with silver buttons, was contriving to look six feet tall as he skillfully maneuvered the perfectly matched pair of bays under the admiring eye of the Honorable Jenny who was seated beside him. The effect was spoiled by an involuntary jerk of the reins as he spied his seething master. He carefully eased the carriage to a halt in the precise spot where Lord Dalton had left it. The tiger's eyes were wide with apprehension as Dalton, slowly, deliberately, came down the marble steps.

"I wasn't wanting Your Lordship's cattle to cool off too much," the tiger volunteered in an attempt to avert the tongue-lashing that was coming.

"I think you can rely on me to see that my horses don't suffer. I did say I'd be right back you may recall. And even if you chose to disregard that—purely from concern for my cattle, of course—can you explain why you decided to take on a passenger?"

"Oh, for heaven's sake!" Jenny intervened, smiling pleasantly. "No need to fly up into the boughs, Lord Dalton. None of this is Jasper's fault."

"I can't explain why that fact fails to surprise me, Miss Blythe."

She ignored the sarcasm. "I've never ridden in a high-perch phaeton, you see. And I can't imagine that there's a more handsome equipage in London. No, in the world."

"No need to overdo it, Miss Blythe. I don't intend to skin my tiger alive. Only to see to it that he doesn't come near my rig for at least a fortnight."

"Now lookee 'ere, sir," the tiger wailed. "That ain't fair, that ain't. I didn't let 'er *drive*."

"That's the truth; he didn't," Jenny offered helpfully. "And I really begged him to let me hold the ribbons. I've never seen such mettlesome bays, Lord Dalton. Or so beautiful a pair. Why, it's like seeing double. I did quite long to drive them. And I not only begged, but wheedled. But Jasper was adamant."

The tiger, though unfamiliar with the word, translated the intent and nodded vigorously. "I said as 'ow she'd have to get Your Lordship's permission," he observed virtuously.

"That's true. So now I'm asking it. When may I drive your phaeton, Lord Dalton?"

"When hell freezes over, Miss Blythe." He held out a gloved hand to help her from the rig. She chose to ignore it, but spoiled the effect by catching her toe in the hem of her pelisse. He caught her as she tumbled.

"That was graceful," he offered as he still held on to her.

"Blast! That thing is high."

"That's why they call it a *high-perch* phaeton," he said witheringly. "And speaking of heights—" It was an odd experience to hold a lady in his arms almost at eye level.

"You do so at your own peril," she retorted, extracting herself from his support, a maneuver that took a surprising effort of will.

"You're prickly about that, aren't you? Damned silly, if you ask me. There are many advantages to being tall."

"For a man, certainly. Well, for a woman, too," she conceded. "Except that every advantage seems to be offset by the fact that ladies are expected to be inferior in every way, including stature. But my size is without doubt an asset when it comes to driving. And, I can assure you, I'm a complete hand."

His look spoke volumes.

"Spare me your skepticism. It's true. But I totally lack the power to persuade you to let me demonstrate. Whereas were I five-feet-nothing and could gaze up at you adoringly, I'm sure you wouldn't hesitate to put the ribbons in my hands. With you giving me the benefit of your *superior skill*, of course. Which I really wouldn't need since I drive quite as well as you, sir."

"In a pig's eye, you do. But never mind that. If it's any comfort, size has nothing to say in the matter. I don't intend to entrust my rig to Lady Sylvia, either."

"I can't imagine that she'd wish you to do so."

"Which is, undoubtedly, a great part of her appeal." He grinned evilly and vaulted up onto the maroon-colored leather seat. "Good day, Miss Blythe." He tipped his curly-brimmed beaver in exaggerated courtesy as he sprang his horses.

"Well, isn't he the regular red-hot tearer," Miss Blythe observed disgustedly to the world at large as his lordship shaved the corner on two wheels.

Chapter Eleven

INSIDE, JENNY WENT in search of her cousins. She found Sylvia in her bedchamber being helped into a becoming walking dress by her abigail. "Our aunt wants me to go with her to pay a call on Lady Jersey. I think she wishes to revel in last night's triumph." Sylvia sounded rather less than delighted at the prospect.

"Well, there's no point in your staying here, since Lord Dalton has already called," Jenny observed, sitting down on the canopied bed. "For, according to Aunt Lydia, if you have him in your pocket, there's no more to be desired. And as much as I hate to agree, she may have a point. Have you seen his high-perch phaeton?"

This produced a chuckle. "You really are awful, Jenny. But you'll not persuade me you're mercenary."

"Not when it comes to jewels, perhaps. But, oh, those bays! You must see them."

"I collect I shall—at five this afternoon—for he's asked to drive me in the park." The abigail withdrew, and Sylvia turned away from the cheval glass. "I was coming to find you before I left to see if you'd go with me."

"Whatever for? You certainly don't need a chaperon to ride in an open carriage with a gentleman."

"Oh, I know that. But I should prefer it."

"Well, our aunt would not. Nor would Lord Dalton. Not that I care a fig for his feelings in the matter. It's yours I don't understand, Sylvia. Have you taken a dislike to Lord Dalton?"

"Oh, no. Nothing like that. It's just—" She hesitated, as if finding it too difficult to put feelings into words. "It's just that I don't wish to be on intimate terms with anyone just yet."

"Well, that is unfortunate, since it's the purpose of this whole come-out exercise."

"I know. But there's no need to rush matters that I can see. Please say you'll come, Jenny. It sounds silly, I know, but it's quite important to me."

There was no ignoring her intensity. Jenny capitulated. "Oh, very well then. But if either our aunt or Lord Dalton murders me, my blood will be on your head."

They were interrupted by their aunt who was, as always, the very picture of fashion in a lavender pelisse with black braided frogs and a matching bonnet. Jenny had to admit that she was still quite stunning, despite her years. It was just as well, she thought, that her own comfortable and countrified parent could not see her. She liked her mother the way she was, despite the fact that she no doubt now looked to be the older sister.

"Oh, good. There you are, Jenny. I had planned to leave word that Sylvia and I are going out and that you and Claire can play hostess to any callers who may come merely to congratulate us on last night's success. It will be good training for you both. And do try and persuade your cousin to be more sociable. Since she has destroyed her beauty through gluttony, she should work particularly hard on her conversation. Come along, Sylvia. We must hurry if you're to be back and changed by five."

Jenny sighed—and waited long enough for the pair to be out of sight. She then went in search of the butler. "Oh, Jackson, if anyone should call, we aren't at home." Perhaps it was only her imagination that he gave her a questioning look. After all, good butlers did not ask for explanations. She also hoped that good butlers did not report everything to their mistresses. It did seem a colossal waste of time for Claire and her to entertain Sylvia's admirers, who invariably made up the majority of their callers. It would be pleasant to have a few moments to themselves.

Jenny went first to her cousin's bedchamber, hoping to pass the good news of their reprieve on to Claire before she fortified herself for the ordeal with chocolates. Although, come to think on it, it did seem that Claire was not as heavy as she had been. Still, it was hard to see how the cracker-water regimen could be helping since regular meals were being smuggled in to her.

Claire was not to be found in her bedchamber. Jenny went from there to the next likely place. Sure enough, she heard piano music as she approached the gold withdrawing room.

It was not her cousin Claire who was playing so beautifully, but Lord Fremantle. Claire was there, however, leaning on the pianoforte with a rapt expression on her face. Jenny looked at them thoughtfully as a startling idea struck her. She was turning

86

to tiptoe away when Claire glanced up and spied her.

"Oh, Jenny! How famous! Do come in. Have you heard our cousin play? He's truly marvelous, isn't he?"

"Why, yes, he is," Jenny heartily agreed. "Do you mind an audience, Cousin?"

"Well . . ." he smiled. "I truly would mind an 'audience,' but I'm certainly glad to have you listen if you're sure you won't be bored."

Jenny was certainly not bored. Although her own compulsory music lessons had borne very little other fruit, she had developed an appreciation for the talents of others. "Oh, that was lovely," she breathed when he'd finished.

"Yes, wasn't it?" Claire turned toward her eagerly. "Did you know that Cousin James has promised to take us to the opera? I can hardly wait."

"How kind of you, Cousin. And did you know that our Claire has an exquisite voice herself?" Jenny felt rather like an overly eager mama with a daughter to launch. She did hope that she didn't sound it.

Lord Fremantle's response was all that she might have wished for. His face beamed with pleasure. "Why, no. You should have told me," he said to Claire. "Can I persuade you to demonstrate? Do you perhaps know 'Robin Adair'?"

Claire did indeed know it, and after he had played it through once by way of prelude, she began to sing in her clear, true soprano. Jenny sat through a verse and then slipped quietly away. The musicians were far too engrossed to notice her departure.

* * *

Lord Dalton did not bother to look pleased that Sylvia had included Jenny in their ride. In fact, Jenny suspected that it was on the tip of his tongue to tell her to stay home, but even Lord Dalton, she collected, would not be that lost to propriety. She returned a sweet smile for the darkling look he gave her.

Nor did he allow her to climb up into his phaeton unassisted, though he did look sorely tempted. But after he'd taken rather longer than necessary in seeing that Sylvia was comfortably settled, he turned and held out a gloved hand. "Do watch your step. I trust you're better at going up than down."

"Oh, don't worry. I've no intention of flinging myself at you again."

"Oh, no? Well, appearances say otherwise."

She might have known, she fumed, as she squeezed in next to Sylvia—who showed little inclination to scoot over, though there was ample room next to his lordship to allow it. The conceited ape believed she was in hot pursuit of him. Oh, well, let him think it. It must be reflex with him at this point, thanks to all the bird-witted females that London seemed to attract.

Lord Dalton appeared completely engrossed by his driving as he skillfully threaded his bays through the heavy traffic. Sylvia was not one to chatter at the best of times. Now she seemed to be put off entirely by his lordship's failure to make conversation. Jenny endured the silence as long as her nature would allow, but as Dalton steered his pair into the park entrance, she leaned across her cousin to inquire, "Have you been in some sort of brawl, sir?"

"A brawl?" He frowned, puzzled. "I don't know

what—Oh." He touched his face gingerly. The skin below his left eye was puffed, beginning to discolor.

"Should I not have called attention to the fact that you've recently been battered?"

"Hardly *battered*, Miss Blythe. In fact, you should see the other cove."

"You've left him bruised and bleeding in some mews, then?"

"Nothing quite so dramatic. I did manage a leveler that took him to the mat. But only momentarily."

"How tame. Whatever happened to pistols at dawn for settling quarrels?"

"No quarrel, Miss Blythe. Sorry to disappoint."

"You came to blows then purely for the fun of it?" Her tone was sarcastic.

"Exactly."

"Well, if you don't choose to explain, I certainly will change the subject."

"Good."

"Surely, Jenny," Sylvia said, "you must by now realize that his lordship has been to visit Gentleman Jackson's."

"And who, pray tell, is Gentleman Jackson?"

"You really are from another planet, aren't you?" Dalton observed.

"Gentleman Jackson has a boxing establishment in Bond street," Sylvia supplied. "Did you strip with Jackson himself, sir?"

"Yes, as a matter of fact, I did." His lordship was thawing.

"That's quite an honor, I understand."

"Why?" Jenny's tone conveyed her lack of appreciation.

"Because"—Dalton assumed the patient expression of a tutor with a backward child—"he's a pugilist. A former champion of England, no less."

"And you knocked him down? He must be well past it, then."

Sylvia tried, unsuccessfully, to stifle a giggle with a white kid glove.

Dalton whipped up his horses—as if eager to get the ride over with as soon as possible.

Chapter Twelve

He was soon forced to slow down, however, for the park teemed with activity. It almost seemed as if all fashionable London was abroad, to see and to be seen. As they proceeded down Rotten Row, they were constantly nodding and waving to acquaintances in curricles, gigs, landaus, and phaetons, as well as passing or being passed by men and women on horseback.

"Oh, how I long to ride," Jenny sighed as they approached an elegant lady in a slate-colored riding habit, accompanied by a corpulent middle-aged gentleman who seemed several stones too heavy for his horse. The gentleman doffed his hat as they drew abreast, but the lady gave Lord Dalton a pointed stare, then cut him dead.

Without hearing the woman's voice, Jenny had no way of actually knowing, but she would have bet a monkey that this was the lady from the cloakroom at Almack's. "A friend of yours, Lord Dalton?" she inquired innocently.

"Obviously not." His lordship's mood was not improving.

Sylvia tactfully changed the subject. "I didn't know that you enjoy riding, Jenny. Perhaps our cousin could mount you."

"No. I hinted, but it seems that Fremantle doesn't keep riding horses in London. I gather he's not fond of the exercise."

"There's always Tattersall's," Lord Dalton offered. "You could hire a mount, you know."

"Not on my allowance."

"Well, now, Miss Blythe, if you're expecting me to offer to mount you, you're in for a disappointment. I've far too much respect for my horses to risk them with a green'un accustomed to empty country lanes. Riding in London is another matter entirely, I assure you. So save your hints for Fremantle."

"I was not hinting." Jenny glared around Sylvia. "I would not dream of doing such a thing. Not only would it be presumptuous, it would also be a waste of time. For as you should recall, I've already experienced your 'generosity' with your cattle. But I can assure you, sir, that I'm an accomplished rider as well as an able whip."

"Indeed? Do remind me to put your name up for the Four-in-Hand Club."

Jenny glanced at her cousin to see how she was taking all this bickering. If she'd hoped that Sylvia might be developing a disgust for his irascible lordship, she was doomed to disappointment. Her cousin appeared oblivious to anything that had been said. Her attention was riveted upon an approaching group of horsemen. She was pale as death. She might have seen a ghost.

The four mounted gentlemen were passing the phaeton, absorbed with their own conversation, when one of them, dressed in the uniform of the Household Brigade, reined in suddenly. "Lady Sylvia!" he exclaimed.

Dalton obligingly pulled his bays to a halt. The young officer rode up beside them while his companions proceeded slowly on down the Row. "I had heard you were in London." The soldier smiled. "But I had despaired of seeing you."

Jenny studied the newcomer with unabashed interest. He was exceedingly handsome, with dark brown hair and eyes and a brave military mustache. And, needless to say, the dashing uniform he wore did nothing to dim his luster. There was no way to account for the effect he was having on Sylvia. She was clearly agitated and made the introductions with difficulty. "May I present Captain St. Laurent?" Her voice shook slightly. "We became acquainted in Vienna. Captain, this is my cousin, Miss Blythe, and our friend, Lord Dalton."

The introductions were acknowledged and Sylvia, doing her obvious best to sound offhand, turned to her companions. "Would you please excuse me to have a private word with Captain St. Laurent? I can't tell you how I long to hear the news from home."

"Of course." Dalton did not look best pleased, but he jumped down and assisted her from the carriage, while the handsome captain dismounted. He then guided the phaeton off the carriage drive and onto the grass, while Sylvia and her friend walked out of earshot, the captain leading his horse by the bridle.

"If you don't wish to keep your horses standing, this would be an excellent time to show me what it would be like to drive a high-perch phaeton."

"I don't mind letting my horses stand."

"But wouldn't it be considerate to allow Sylvia time alone with her friend? They obviously have a great deal to say to each other." She looked back over her shoulder to where the twosome stood. The usually reticent Sylvia seemed to be talking a mile a minute while she gazed earnestly up into the captain's face. The soldier had released his horse. It was cropping the dried grass nearby. "I think it would be tactful to drive on."

"I'm not noted for my tact, Miss Blythe."

"How you amaze me. The captain's a handsome fellow, isn't he?" A wide smile brightened her face.

"You're really enjoying this, aren't you?"

"Frankly, yes. I dare say this is the first time in your heartbreaking career that you've been left to cool your heels while your lady enjoyed a tête-à-tête with another gentleman."

"Never mind all that. Who is he, anyhow?"

"I haven't the slightest idea."

That was not strictly true. She did have her suspicions. Ever since Claire had first intimated to her that Sylvia seemed reluctant to make an entrée into Society, they'd often speculated about the cause. Their favorite theory had been that Sylvia was already in love with someone. This incident gave some real substance to their surmise. St. Laurent certainly looked like a likely candidate. It was easy to imagine any female losing her heart to him.

Dalton was imagining just that. And while the possibility didn't cause him any painful heartburnings, he did find the situation irritating. It was ironic, at the very least, after maneuvering for years to avoid the marriage trap set for him by love-smitten and/or mercenary females and their mamas, that once he'd finally decided to take the fatal step, he should find the going so confounded rough.

He was sorely tempted to give up on Lady Sylvia.

Except for her astonishing beauty, he did not find much about her to interest him. But she was his father's choice. And pleasing his dying father was now his lordship's main concern. Besides, the man who had just floored the former boxing champion of all England was highly competitive. He did not approve of being second best.

"Well, well. It is true then, that one sees everyone one knows on Rotten Row whether one wishes it or not."

Jenny's disgusted tone pulled Dalton out of his reverie. He glanced over his shoulder, in the direction she was looking, and saw Chalgrove cantering their way. He reined in by Sylvia and the captain and dismounted. "Were we speaking of tact?" Jenny inquired of no one in particular. "So much for privacy."

"One doesn't come to Hyde Park for privacy. You can't fault Chalgrove for his sociability."

"Oh, you're quite wrong there, Lord Dalton. I can fault Mr. Chalgrove for anything."

"You still haven't forgiven him I see. Small wonder, perhaps. But tell me, Miss Blythe. Have you met anyone in London you do approve of?"

"A few."

"Would you care to enumerate? I'm agog to know who these paragons might be."

"Well, my cousin Fremantle, for one."

"Hmm. We've been acquainted for years, but I'll confess I don't know him all that well."

"No, you wouldn't. He lacks your—dash."

" 'Dash'? Well, since you were at an obvious loss for words I won't belabor the point. Indeed, I confess I expected worse. But I was going on to say I don't doubt that Fremantle possesses sterling qualities. Who else has made your list?"

"There's Mr. York-Jones for another. I don't know about 'sterling qualities,' though. I suspect he's too much under Mr. Chalgrove's thumb to possess many of those. But he is delightfully amusing. I like him prodigiously."

"And I understand he's quite smitten."

"With me? Fustian."

"No, I have it on the best authority. Everyone's remarking on it."

"*Snickering* on it, more likely."

"Well you aren't the conventional couple, you must agree."

"We aren't any kind of 'couple.' But I am thinking seriously of him for Cousin Sylvia. I think they'd deal well together. Tell me, is he as rich as you are?"

"Near enough." Dalton refused to rise to bait.

It appeared that Mr. Chalgrove had brought the reunion to a halt. He now escorted Sylvia back to the phaeton.

Dalton greeted him with a sardonic smile. "Ah, the ubiquitous Mr. Chalgrove. And to think I only used to see you at White's—or perhaps Brook's—when we're both in funds. What brings you to the park today?"

"Why, the beautiful weather." Chalgrove looked upward at the glowering skies that threatened a downpour at any moment. "And of course the need for exercise."

"It's beyond my ken," Jenny offered to no one in particular, "why certain persons refer to riding as 'exercise.' Surely the horse does all the work."

"Miss Blythe puts me in my place as usual."

Chalgrove's smile was patently artificial. "You're looking especially charming today. That cherry color becomes you. But perhaps I should also complement Lady Sylvia. Your aunt informs me that she chooses all your clothes."

It was on the tip of Jenny's tongue to inform him that she'd brought this particular pelisse from home when she realized how childish that would sound. She must stop allowing every word he uttered make her hackles rise. She returned a smile fully as false as his. "My cousin and I *both* thank you," she replied.

"If you slide over a bit, Miss Blythe, I'll hand Lady Sylvia up."

It seemed awkward not to comply and make Sylvia clamber over her. Jenny slid.

And it seemed to her that petite Sylvia was taking up altogether too much room on the carriage seat, for Jenny was jammed, shoulder and thigh, up against his lordship, a fact that did not seem to please that gentleman overly much.

And what was worse, as she had ample time to discover on the long ride home, the proximity was more than a bit unsettling to her own sensibilities.

Chapter Thirteen

THE FOLLOWING MORNING Jenny watched from an upstairs window as her cousin Sylvia, enveloped in a heavy cloak against the bitter chill, hurried down the street. The weather did not seem conducive to exercise. Nor was Sylvia in the habit of taking early walks. And, what was more, Sylvia had ventured forth alone.

But it wasn't the fact that her aunt would fly into the boughs at the mere thought of such impropriety that caused Jenny to snatch her own cloak and hurry out-of-doors. She fully admitted to herself that she was consumed with curiosity.

Sylvia was nowhere in sight as she hurried along Charles Street. But as she rounded the corner she saw her up ahead, still walking at a prodigious clip. I should be ashamed of myself, Jenny scolded silently, for spying on my cousin. But her conscience refused to respond properly.

Jenny kept a considerable distance between herself and Sylvia, in the meantime picking spots to duck out of sight in case her cousin suddenly turned around. She also tried to think what she might say if she were discovered skulking along behind her cousin. Oh, Sylvia, I didn't see you up ahead, sounded rather lame.

Every instinct told her that this exercise had something to do with the handsome captain they had met yesterday in the park. For it was totally unlike her conventional cousin to set out alone this way. It had to mean an assignation. Jenny slowed her pace on Mount Street as she realized that the destination must be the circulating library. A "chance encounter" in such a place would be above reproach.

She dawdled outside, thinking regretfully of the books she might have returned if she had only known. But after having given ample time for Sylvia perhaps to consider it coincidence if she were spied entering the place, she strolled nonchalantly inside.

She went directly to the watercolor table, as though intent upon a purchase. Sylvia must not suspect she was being followed. Jenny glanced furtively about the room, where a sprinkling of customers were browsing among the items for sale. Her cousin wasn't there. She must have gone on into the library proper. Jenny chose a box of paints to account for her presence, then discovered that in her haste she'd forgotten her reticule. "Oh, blast!" she muttered.

"Tsk, tsk. Out of funds?" a sympathetic voice murmured behind her. She clutched her heart.

"Mr. Chalgrove!" she said crossly. "You startled me out of my wits."

"Oh? Jumpy, are we?" The gentleman smiled mockingly. He was looking unusually dapper in a rust-colored coat and pale lemon, tight-fitting pantaloons with matching buttons marching up the sides of his muscular legs. But Jenny was in no mood to appreciate sartorial splendor.

" 'Jumpy'? Not in the least," she retorted. "It's just that you slipped up behind me. What was it Lord Dalton called you? *Ubiquitous?*"

"Oh, there's no secret as to why I'm here, Miss Blythe. In fact, I can safely say that my objective is the same as yours."

"Indeed? I'd no idea that you are a watercolorist, Mr. Chalgrove."

"I'm not. You and I share another interest entirely."

"I haven't the faintest notion of what that might possibly be."

"Oh, I think you have, Miss Blythe. We both seem to share a penchant for spying."

The look she gave him was intended to be withering. He merely laughed. "It's a pity females aren't addicted to quizzing glasses. They are no end helpful when it comes to setdown looks." To prove his point he leveled his glass at her and imitated her expression.

"I know you have a reputation for wit, sir, but your humor eludes me."

"Then I beg pardon." He bowed mockingly. "And to atone for my sins I'll save you a bit of bother. Your cousin is in the next room, pulling volume after volume off the shelves . . . as though intent upon selecting a book for herself. Captain St. Laurent, who was here some fifteen minutes before her and kept consulting his watch nervously all that time, is going through the same book-hunting charade. But actually, they're in earnest conversation."

"Indeed? Well, I'm amazed that you aren't behind them eavesdropping."

"I would be if there were places for concealment within earshot."

"You, sir, are shameless."

"And you, Miss Blythe, are not entirely above reproach."

"You are also presumptuous. Sylvia and I are actually together. She simply came on ahead when I had to run back home a moment."

"To get your reticule, perhaps?"

"My reasons are not your concern, sir. Nor is it any business of yours if my cousin should chance to encounter an old family friend."

"That's true. Nor is it my concern that this is no chance encounter. You see, I happened to hear her ask the captain—quite urgently—to meet her here. And since it seemed unlike Lady Sylvia to behave so . . . oddly, I was motivated to discover what was going on. Though I must confess I'm still no wiser. Except that they're obviously much more than mere acquaintances. Perhaps you might enlighten me."

"I've already told you. He's a dear family friend."

"In other words, this business is as mysterious to you as it is to me. I suspected as much when you came skulking in here." He pulled his watch from its pocket and consulted it. "Well, now, Miss Blythe. I think we should be going."

" 'We' will do nothing of the sort."

"Well, I don't intend to embarrass her ladyship with my presence. I merely wished to satisfy my curiosity, not put her to the blush. And I really think it would be considerate of you to do the same. I don't think we should count on their being inside the library much longer. It could be noticed by the other book lovers. So shall I pay for that box of watercolors you're clutching?"

"That isn't necessary." Jenny put the box back down on the table. She hated to admit that he had a point, but she certainly didn't wish to be discovered by her cousin. Chalgrove opened the outer door for her with a flourish and they stepped outside.

"You don't need to escort me, sir," she said pointedly as they set out together.

"We are going in the same direction," he answered reasonably. "I could, of course, fall several paces behind you. But it seems a bit absurd. Could we not call a truce, Miss Blythe?"

"Why ever should we?"

He sighed. "Yours is certainly an unforgiving nature. I long ago repented of my sinful remark at Almack's."

"Good. But that's no reason we should become bosom bows."

"I don't ask for that. But is it necessary to be at daggers drawn?"

"Mr. Chalgrove"—she stopped in the middle of the walkway—"you are, they tell me, greatly admired by the fashionable world. And I understand that it's necessary to have your good opinion—or at least not to incur your ill opinion—if one is to be accepted by that fashionable world. Well, I must tell you, sir, that I don't give a fig about that world. And I certainly will not believe that you give a fig for my good opinion."

"But that's where you're wrong, my dear lady. I do care. Quite a few figs in fact."

"Whatever for?" she demanded.

"That's simple enough to answer. You're Lady Sylvia's cousin. She admires you greatly. And I greatly fear that I'm falling in love with her."

He tipped his beaver and gave a courtly bow. She stood rooted and gazed after him, mouth agape, as he strolled jauntily on down Mount Street.

Chapter Fourteen

JENNY HAD BEEN so preoccupied with Sylvia's affairs that she had paid little mind to Claire. But as she went into her cousin's bedchamber to borrow a pair of eardrops for the opera, it occurred to her that Claire was looking quite nice indeed.

She was seated at her dressing table while the abigail made a final adjustment to her coiffure. And though far from slender, Claire had surely lost some weight, Jenny concluded as she observed her closely. The change was most evident in her face, which had lost a great deal of its puffiness. The skillful maid was helping the cause along by ignoring the current fashion that called for ringlets before the ears, broadening the face even further. She had swept Claire's lustrous blond locks upward to the crown and tied the gathered curls with a ribbon. The effect was charming. But the biggest change was in Claire's expression. She seemed alight.

"Oh, you do look nice," Jenny blurted out.

Claire rose and regarded herself in the looking glass. "It is a nice gown, isn't it?" she said, turning this way and that. "Sylvia does have excellent taste, does she not? She seems to know exactly what a fat person should and shouldn't wear."

"Oh, for goodness sake, Claire! Can't you learn to accept a simple compliment? I said *you* look nice. I wasn't speaking of Sylvia's taste in gowns. And I certainly was not making any reference to your weight. You know, you really can be most exasperating."

"Well, then, thank you, Cousin." Claire dropped an exaggerated curtsy. "Now, is that better?"

"Much, thank you." Jenny smiled. "I've come to borrow your pearl eardrops. That is, if you don't mind."

"As a matter of fact, I do." Claire was studying Jenny's cream-colored gown thoughtfully. "I think my garnets would suit better." She rummaged in her jewelry box, produced them, and held one up to her cousin's ear. "Oh, yes. I was right. These will be the very thing. See?" She laughed. "I haven't watched our cousin Sylvia in action for all this time and learned nothing."

"Heaven help me," Jenny groaned as she fastened the jewels in her ears and stood back to survey the results. "I'm sure you're right. But how I'm going to survive two arbiters of fashion is beyond me. I'll never be allowed to leave the house."

"You goosecap. It's just that I wish this evening to be absolutely perfect. In every detail. Oh, Jenny, I can't tell you how excited I am. I've longed all my life to attend the opera. Isn't it famous of Cousin James to take us?"

"Oh, yes, indeed." Jenny refrained from saying that at least a half-dozen other gentlemen had made the same offer. She, too, wanted Claire's evening to be perfect.

* * *

It had been Lord Fremantle's intent to limit the opera evening to a family party. His stepmama was having none of that, however. First and foremost, Lord Dalton must be included for Sylvia. Mr. York-Jones would do for Jenny. Their disparate heights did make them an absurd-looking couple, but they seemed to get on well together and York-Jones could be depended upon to enliven the dullest of parties. What's more, his antecedents were impeccable. His father had fallen head over heels in love with her in '97. And, she mused on, Sir Bertram Philpott, the spotty young man from Almack's, would do nicely for Claire. That left Lord Fremantle, of course, to be her escort. If her stepson found any fault with these arrangements, he kept it strictly to himself.

Jenny, however, was not so biddable. On the way to the Haymarket she managed to put a flea in York-Jones's ear. So when they took their places in a box overlooking the stage of the opera house, she somehow managed to commandeer Sir Bertram—while York-Jones firmly attached himself to Lady Fremantle. This left the two music lovers together to enjoy the performance.

She was only sorry that the twosome were relegated to the back of the box along with herself and her overawed escort. Fremantle had at least seen to it that Claire sat behind petite Sylvia, and she declared, with shining eyes, that she had a wonderful view of the stage. Lord Dalton had then obligingly offered her his seat, but under the influence of Jenny's glare had not insisted when Claire politely refused the trade.

Jenny took advantage of the opera glasses that her host provided to drink in the grandeur of the building. It had been redone by Nash and Repton only a few years previously and was a tribute to their superior taste and style. She quickly counted five tiers of boxes, surmounted by a gallery, then turned to admire the proportions of the enormous stage with the orchestra recessed in front of it. She noted the painted horse and chariot galloping on clouds within the dome and the intricate plaster work that ringed this ceiling painting. After admiring the rich red curtains and the candelabra that extended in rows above the boxes, she then felt free to peruse the audience.

She was marveling at all the finery—the plumes, the jewels, the gowns that surely even Paris could not surpass—when her glass ceased its pilgrimage with a sudden jerk, then leaped back to confirm what it had just glimpsed.

Sure enough, there sat Mr. Chalgrove in the same tier, almost opposite them, across the wide expanse of auditorium. And it came as no surprise that he was surveying their party through his quizzing glass. She quickly lowered her own glass, feeling a bit foolish. But she had already identified his partner. It was the haughty beauty from the park, the lady who had cut Lord Dalton dead.

The orchestra struck up the overture just then, but failed to capture Jenny's attention. She kept thinking about Mr. Chalgrove across the way. There was no use pretending that his presence here was mere coincidence. It was obvious that he was following Sylvia. Jenny was not at all pleased with this further evidence of his devotion. She soon succumbed to the magic taking place onstage, however, and by the first interval was almost as enraptured as Claire.

The party then decided to leave their box and stretch their legs a bit. Jenny was surprised to find Lord Dalton at her elbow. Sylvia had joined Sir Bertram and was concerned with setting the awkward young man at ease, which Jenny, in her preoccupation, had failed to do. "Enjoying yourself, Miss Blythe?" Dalton inquired politely as they strolled behind the other two down the crowded corridor.

"Why, yes, as a matter of fact," she answered. "And you?"

"Let's just say that I find *Figaro* less of a dead bore than most operas. And I've had other things as well to intrigue me."

"Indeed? I trust you plan to elaborate."

"Most assuredly. I've become somewhat accustomed to your high-handedness. And I'm well aware that you bear-lead your cousins shamelessly—"

"I do no such thing!" she interrupted.

"Shamelessly. You put even the most scheming mamas I have met—and believe me, I've met quite a few of them—to the blush. So I was most admiring of the way you sorted out our party, commandeering young Bertram and palming York-Jones off onto your aunt. All in aid of seeing to it that Fremantle and your cousin Claire could be together. Am I right?"

"Absolutely. And I'm not the least bit ashamed of it."

"I didn't suppose you would be."

"Fremantle arranged this outing for Claire's benefit. They are both talented musicians. It was only fair that they enjoy the performance together."

"Oh, I heartily concur. But what surprises me is

108

that you failed to separate Lady Sylvia and myself. Don't tell me it proved too much for your generalship. I'll be sorely disappointed. Why, there are all sorts of possibilities. You could have attached yourself to me, leaving Lady Sylvia to deal with Sir Bertram. Which she's doing famously, isn't she?" He looked admiringly at the couple ahead. The young man had emerged from his shell and was talking a mile a minute. "Look at her. She appears to be hanging on that young pup's every word."

"She doesn't 'appear to be,' she is. I told you that Sylvia is nice."

"All the more puzzling why you didn't try and come between us this evening."

"To be quite candid—"

"Are you ever otherwise?"

"To be candid, I thought parting you two might well be the final straw where my aunt's good nature was concerned. But more to the point, I wasn't sure it was advisable."

"My God!" He came to a sudden halt. A gentleman behind bumped into him and apologized. "Don't tell me I've gained your approval?"

"Well . . ." she temporized, "let's just say you're the lesser evil. I think you're to be preferred over your chief rival."

" 'Chief rival'?" He looked puzzled for a moment. "Oh, you mean Chalgrove."

"I'm afraid so."

"It's odd. He was never in the petticoat line before, but he does appear to be smitten. He's certainly developed the habit of turning up everywhere we go."

"Then you know he's here tonight."

"Oh, yes, indeed. And I also know who's with

him." He looked grim. "I've been expecting a visit momentarily. That's the sort of thing Chalgrove has always delighted in—throwing the cat among the pigeons, as it were. Heretofore he's never needed a reason to make mischief. God knows the lengths he may go to in order to put me out of the running." He grinned suddenly. "This should prove interesting."

"I don't see anything amusing in the situation. I certainly don't wish my cousin to become entangled with him."

"I hope this doesn't mean you're about to sponsor me in the lists. Something tells me that could be fatal. Or perhaps I just have a natural aversion to becoming one of your pawns."

"I wouldn't dream of pushing your suit." She grimaced with distaste. "Just because I find you preferable to Mr. Chalgrove doesn't mean I think you'd be ideal husband material. Of course"—she brightened up—"if you two become rivals and go to any lengths to cut each other out, there's always the chance Sylvia may form a disgust of you both."

"How charming of you to point the possibility out." He dropped his bantering tone and turned serious. "I shouldn't wonder if we're neither one in the running, though. I'll own I'm more than a bit curious about the military cove she met in the park when we took our drive. She seemed most upset by the encounter. I wonder if he's the rival I should fear, not Chalgrove. What do you think, Miss Blythe?"

Sylvia and Sir Bertram turned at that moment to join them, and Jenny was prevented from having to reply. Which was just as well, for she hadn't the slightest notion of how to answer Dalton. She, too, was convinced that there was a romantic involvement between Sylvia and the military stranger. She was also convinced that the handsome soldier had to be in some way unsuitable or Sylvia would not be tearing herself apart over him, as was so obviously the case.

Lord Dalton and Sir Bertram changed places as they strolled back to their box. Jenny was too preoccupied to do the polite, and Sir Bertram lost all his newly acquired vivaciousness. At the second interval, Dalton's prediction came true. Mr. Chalgrove arrived at the Fremantle box just as the party had risen to leave it. Jenny gazed curiously but, she hoped, covertly at the lady with him. Though well beyond the first blush of youth, she was certainly handsome, fairly tall, although not in Jenny's class, with titian hair, and hazel eyes bordering on green. She was beautifully and expensively dressed and fairly blazed with diamonds. Jenny wondered if the elaborate necklace that she wore was intended to draw attention away from—or to—her rather daring décolletage.

There was no need to present Lady Warrington to Lord and Lady Fremantle or Lord Dalton, to whom Lady Warrington gave only the briefest of nods. But she declared herself in raptures at finally meeting the three cousins. "I can't tell you how I've longed to know the celebrated Percival progeny. I can assure you, London talks of little else."

I don't doubt it for a minute, Jenny thought darkly. And I'll wager that Lord Dalton's castaway is about to tell us exactly what they're saying.

"Now let me sort you out," Lady Warrington continued. "You're one of the twins' daughters, am I not right?" She smiled falsely at Jenny, who merely nodded. "But surely the resemblance is slight? At least I can't recall it being said that the Percivals were above the average. Oh, dear. I did not mean— What a rackety thing to say." Her laugh was brittle. "I referred only to stature, needless to say. You must have inherited your height from your father."

"No, ma'am. My father, like the Percivals, is little above the average. I'm the family anomaly." Jenny's smile was fully as false as her ladyship's.

"Now, then, let me see." Lady Warrington turned her attention to Claire. "You're Lord Hazlett's daughter, then. I find it so charming the way he quite dotes on the little ones. But then I collect it's quite typical of gentlemen who come to fatherhood late in life. It's pride in their own prowess that makes them so foolish over their offspring I've no doubt."

Lady Fremantle gave a little gasp. Lord Fremantle did not change expression, but moved a bit closer to Lady Claire. Dalton could have been contemplating murder, while Mr. Chalgrove, for possibly the first time in his life, looked out of countenance.

"I—I beg pardon," Claire stammered, "but I've really no notion of what you're talking about."

Jenny, all too aware of the currents swirling around them, quickly intervened. "I think you've confused me and my cousin, Lady Warrington. It's *my* father who has the young children. And, yes, he is extremely foolish over them. But I'm not at all sure that age is a factor. He actually dotes on us older ones as well."

"My mistake." Lady Warrington looked well satisfied with the effect she was creating. But she had been saving her best for last. "And I'm particularly delighted to meet you at last, Lady Sylvia. All London seems to be at your feet. Why, I understand you've even managed to enslave Dalton here. How odd to hear he's lost his heart when it was the consensus that he didn't have one. But then, when one has been on the town as long as he has and played the field so tirelessly, I suppose he was finally bound to settle down—from sheer fatigue." Her laugh appeared to taunt him. He stared back at her with folded arms, his face expressionless. "But it is quite plain, Lady Sylvia," she continued, "that you're destined to perpetuate the legend of the beautiful Percival sisters . . . who cast all those poor, unfortunate debutantes of their Season in the shade."

"Oh, come now, Lady Warrington, I'm sure that you exaggerate." Jenny smiled. "I know the Percivals had a reputation for beauty, but I'll not believe that they could cast *you* in the shade."

There was a pregnant silence. Then the Honorable York-Jones snickered. Two bright spots, not accounted for by the rouge pot, burned on Lady Warrington's cheeks. "If you are implying that I was present at that come-out, I can assure you I was in leading strings at the time."

"Oh, dear. Really? Well then I have made a faux pas, haven't I? You must forgive me. The mistake is understandable. It's not that you look so very old, Lady Warrington, it's just that our aunt here looks so very young. It totally confuses one's perspective."

"Well, Emily, m'dear," Mr. Chalgrove murmured, "the orchestra is tuning up. I do believe we should be going and leave the field in Miss Blythe's possession." And with a rueful backward look at Lady Sylvia, who returned it with one of deep reproach, he whisked Lady Warrington from the box.

"What a perfectly odious female." Lord Fremantle seemed to speak for them all.

"Yes, but our Miss Blythe certainly spiked her guns." York-Jones grinned appreciatively.

"Indeed she did!" Lady Fremantle nodded with satisfaction, setting the purple plumes that adorned her hair into vigorous motion. "I may have reproved you in the past for your unruly tongue, Jenny, but this time I must applaud you. Lady Warrington richly deserved the setdown. I only regret it wasn't worse."

Jenny smiled rather weakly. While it was certainly refreshing to be in her aunt's good graces for a change, she could almost wish she might recall the words she'd spoken. She glanced at Lord Dalton, whose granite face, she was quite sure, masked a seething fury. She suspected that losing him was punishment enough for the spiteful Emily Warrington. It had been quite superfluous to drive another stake into that lady's heart.

Chapter Fifteen

THE COUSINS COULD by this time have written their own tourist's guide to London. Jenny's sight-seeing program had been quite a success, from the Tower of London to an exhibition in the Royal Academy. The various young men whom she'd recruited on the day after their introduction to Almack's had, for the most part, proved delightful escorts. Now it was the turn of Lord Dalton and Astley's Royal Circus.

Jenny thought he'd made an odd choice and called up to him to say so. He merely shrugged and waited a moment to answer as he guided his barouche between a loaded cart that had stopped without any warning and an oncoming yellow-and-black hackney.

Others might find it rather eccentric for his lordship to serve as his own coachman, with his tiger as postillion, but Jenny could not find it in her heart to blame him. Not only did it spare him the necessity of entertaining three females, the carriage itself must be a joy to drive. It was fit for royalty. She was almost inclined to nod and wave at the pedestrians that stared their way as they tooled down Piccadilly.

"I had thought you needed a rest after all that

culture," Dalton said over his shoulder once he'd completed his deft maneuver through the traffic.

The cousins were soon delighted with his choice. After they'd taken their places on the second tier, which afforded the best possible view of the extravaganza, Claire declared that the amphitheater was almost as elegant as the opera house, high praise indeed from her.

Lord Dalton, mindful of his role as tour guide, informed them that the stage was the largest in England, a necessity for the grand spectacles performed there. Astley's was also particularly proud of its lighting. A magnificent glass chandelier was suspended over the circular arena and contained no less than fifty patent lamps.

The audience was certainly more diverse than at the opera. People of all classes were crowded into the huge theater. And there were, of course, a large number of children, transformed into jumping jacks with anticipation. Their excitement seemed contagious, for the crowd as a whole was boisterous though good-natured.

"Oh, this does look like fun!" Jenny leaned across Sylvia to smile gratefully at Lord Dalton. It was only later on that the genuineness of his returning smile seemed surprising.

She soon forgot all else as the performance began with an exhibition of trick riding. Equestrians dashed around the ring performing death-defying acrobatics while the audience gasped and cheered. Then, as a change of pace, a lovely young lady draped in transparent gauze danced like a second Taglioni on the back of a white circus horse. Jenny stole another glance at Dalton. His eyes were glued upon the performer. No wonder he prefers this to opera, she thought.

Lord Dalton's party were soon holding their sides, convulsed with laughter at the antics of the celebrated clown, John Ducrow, who did a series of somersaults on horseback before drinking the contents of a bottle, because he'd been told to "pour it into a tumbler." There was a pause between acts and Jenny was looking forward to the next event, advertised as the "Wild Horse of Tartary," an equestrian drama based on a Byron poem, when Claire suddenly clutched her arm.

"Look down there," she hissed.

Jenny obediently leaned over the balcony to gaze downward into the pit. She fully expected to see Mr. Chalgrove, though the circus hardly seemed his cup of tea. Her eyes scanned the crowd, back and forth, but she saw nothing to account for her cousin's distress. "What is it, Claire?" she whispered.

"There on the front row. Don't you see him?"

Jenny followed Claire's stare, riveted upon an area opposite the recessed stage and just behind a low barrier that framed the ring. She appeared to be looking at a man and two small children. The man, whose thinning hair was the most evident thing about him from their vantage point, had his arm around a female toddler who was standing on the bench beside him so that she could see. A slightly older boy, dressed in a short coat and pantaloons, was leaning rather perilously over the rail. As Jenny watched, the man, obviously a gentleman from the cut of his dark blue coat, pulled the lad back to safety.

"I still don't see what—"

Claire cut her off. "It's Papa," she choked.

Jenny hadn't seen her uncle for years. Certainly Lord Hazlett had had more hair. "Are you sure?" she whispered back.

"Of course I'm sure!" Claire snapped. "I should certainly know my own father."

"From this angle?" Jenny received a withering glare.

Sylvia looked curiously toward her cousins. But as she opened her mouth to speak, she was cut off by a tremendous clap of thunder. This was followed by a rapid succession of fiery streaks of lightning, then a deafening crescendo of thunder. Rain and hail came down in torrents amid what the broadsides had described as the carnage of battle, with wheeling, rearing horses and riders, shouts and bloodcurdling screams, and the clash of sword on sword.

As far as Jenny was concerned, the spectacle was a total waste. She was far too engaged in watching Claire watch the gentleman and his charges below them. The little girl had clapped her hands upon her ears and, apparently, was crying. Lord Hazlett appeared to be trying to comfort her. The lad was made of sterner stuff. He stamped and shouted and cheered with the rest of the audience while the battle raged.

Claire's distress was patent. In order to relieve it, Jenny wracked her brain for acceptable reasons that could account for Hazlett's presence in London and his failure to get in touch with his daughter. *Perhaps he doesn't know she's here.* She quickly dismissed that thought as highly unlikely.

As for the children with him— Well, there were all sorts of explanations for that, she told herself, trying to hold the worst of her imagination at bay.

They could be the children of a friend. Or a servant, when it came to that. Lord Hazlett was fond of children, as she recalled. He'd been most avuncular with her and her siblings on his long-ago visit to their home.

But the odious Lady Warrington's insinuations came back to haunt her. And what was it that Chalgrove had said at their aunt's ball? Surely he, too, had made sly references to Lord Hazlett.

The amphitheater spectacle seemed to be working its way toward a happy ending. The music had softened from its previous blaring frenzy to sweet, melodic strains. Below them, the gentleman with the thinning hair gathered his charges, apparently wishing to whisk them away in advance of the crowd. As he turned slightly to envelop the small girl in a cloak suggestive of Red Riding Hood, Jenny saw his face clearly. She could no longer doubt that it was, indeed, her uncle. As his party began to ease its way out past the knees of the other spectators, Claire stood up suddenly and headed for the exit. "We'll be right back," Jenny whispered hurriedly to Sylvia and followed her.

Claire raced down the stairs and out into the street with Jenny at her heels. They were just in time to see Lord Hazlett lift the children into a waiting carriage and give the coachman a signal to drive on.

"I have to know where he's taking them." Claire sounded desperate. "Do you understand, Jenny? I *have* to know."

Jenny nodded and looked frantically around for a hackney. There was none in sight. "I could go fetch Dalton," she offered.

"I don't want anyone else to know about this. Oh, Jenny, they'll soon be out of sight."

Desperate times call for desperate measures. Jenny turned toward the queue of carriages just beginning to form in anticipation of the end of the performance. Sure enough, Lord Dalton's barouche was second in line. "Come on!" She dragged Claire by the hand. Jack was holding the mettlesome horses by a bridle and talking to them soothingly as the two young women came rushing up. "Get in," Jenny ordered Claire, then turned toward the tiger. "We want you to follow that carriage. It's a matter of life or death."

Jack looked alarmed. "Where's 'is Lordship?" he demanded.

"He's staying till the end of the performance. Now hurry up. We can be back by the time the place empties."

"Lor', miss, it would be as good as me life if I was to drive 'is Lordship's rig without 'is by your leave. Why, 'e 'ardly lets me—"

"Oh, do hurry," Claire wailed, and Jenny reacted. "Well, I can't stand here arguing."

Before the tiger realized what was happening, Jenny had climbed up upon the box and was snaking his lordship's whip out over the horses' heads, where it exploded in an ear-splitting crack.

"Now see 'ere, miss!" the tiger yelled. He made the mistake of releasing the bridle and starting toward her. The horses sprang around the gig in front and out into the street as if pursued by devils. Jack instinctively made a flying leap and landed on the boot as the barouche sped by.

"Oh, do be quiet or else jump off!" Jenny shouted at him as the young man continued to voice his protest at maximum lung power. "We aren't going to harm his lordship's precious carriage."

The tiger might have found this reassuring if at that very moment they hadn't been sideswiped by a curricle coming in the opposite direction.

"You bleedin' nincompoop!" Jack screeched.

"That wasn't my fault!" Jenny shouted indignantly. "That driver was obviously castaway."

"I was yellin' at 'im, not you," the tiger bellowed. " 'e almost knocked me off me perch. Which would 'ave saved 'is Lordship the trouble of murdering me—which 'e's plainly going to do."

As they turned off Westminster Bridge Road, Jenny slowed her team. Lord Hazlett's carriage was in full sight now, proceeding at a sedate pace, illuminated more by the full moon than by the flickering streetlamps.

Jenny kept her distance. Though she didn't think her uncle would know her from Adam's off-ox, she had no doubt that the sight of a young lady in evening dress—tooling a barouche down The Strand—would rivet his attention. No need to take the chance.

When it became obvious that they were headed to Covent Garden, Jack was heard from once again. "Might just as well 'ave jumped off Westminster Bridge and been done with it," he offered to the world at large.

"Don't be absurd," Jenny scoffed. "We'll be perfectly safe."

She would not allow herself to think of the shocking escapade she was engaged in. She did, however, close some of the gap between her and the carriage she was following. From the glimpse she'd had,

Lord Hazlett's burly coachman looked far abler to cope with footpads than their diminutive tiger.

She was more relieved than she cared to admit—even to herself—when they turned into Russel Street. Her newly acquired knowledge of London told her that they were around the corner from Bow Street, the home of the metropolitan law enforcers. The same comforting thought had occurred to Jack. "I 'opes them Runners is in earshot," he offered.

The carriage ahead was slowing up. It came to a complete halt before a row of modest houses. Jenny drove several yards on past it and then pulled to a stop in the shadows. She turned around to look down on Claire. "What do we do now?" she asked.

Chapter Sixteen

"LET'S WAIT HERE till he comes out."

Jenny opened her mouth to debate the wisdom of this course of action, but one look at Claire's miserable face stopped her cold. "If that's what you want," she answered.

Jack was not so compliant. He kept muttering to himself. "Never mind what could 'appen to a cove with two dotty females parked on a dark street in the middle of the night; it ain't even a circumstance compared to what 'is Lordship's gonna do to me. Being given the sack without a proper reference will be the least of it."

"Oh, do be quiet!" Jenny snapped, her nerves rubbed raw. "If Lord Dalton discharges you, I'll ask my father to take you on."

"And where is 'e, miss?"

"Birmingham."

"I'd as lief be dead, then," the tiger muttered glumly.

Time seemed at a standstill. Except for a carriage or two that rattled by, Russel Street was quiet. And cold. Perched upon the box, Jenny thought longingly of the many-caped greatcoats that other coach drivers seemed to favor. Her evening cloak was patently inadequate. As surely

123

Claire's was. "Don't you think we should go?" she asked diffidently.

"He's bound to come out soon," was the taut reply.

But when the last light had flickered out in the last window, Jenny had no choice. "Claire, he isn't coming out. We really must go now. I fear I've kept the horses standing far too long as it is."

"I know." Claire sounded close to tears. "Sylvia and Lord Dalton must be thinking we're never coming back for them."

"Claire," Jenny answered patiently, "we've been gone for ages. They won't still be waiting at the amphitheater."

Lord Dalton was, in fact, waiting outside of Fremantle House when Jenny drove slowly up the street. He had taken the greatly perturbed Lady Sylvia home in a hackney coach and had been pacing rapidly up and down in order to keep warm. He was, however, now leaning against a portico column with folded arms and a face like thunder as Jenny pulled his team to a decorous halt.

"You go on in," she said, speaking softly to Claire. "I'll handle this."

"No, it's all my fault. I'll stay."

"No, you won't. You're on the verge of tears—and the last thing Dalton needs right now is a weepy female. Besides, he can't eat me, can he?"

Jenny soon decided that Lord Dalton was capable of doing just that. He didn't spare a glance for Claire as she hurried past him. His eyes were boring straight through her.

Jack had leaped down from the boot and was holding the horses. Lord Dalton, arms still folded, murderous look still firmly in place, stood by his rig and stared up at the "coachman." "Did you enjoy your trip, Miss Blythe?" he inquired with counterfeit pleasantness.

"Not particularly. And I'm well aware that I owe you an apology."

"For leaving us stranded? For upsetting your cousin, who thought you had been kidnaped? A circumstance I myself felt highly unlikely, by the by. An apology seems most magnanimous of you."

Jenny sighed. She might as well get the worst over with. "Yes, and for scratching your carriage."

"Oh, my God!" Dalton stepped back to survey the damage. "Well, I collect I'm fortunate to even get the thing back at all," he said bitterly. "It could be in complete splinters."

"Oh, I say, guv," Jack piped up, still clinging to the bridle, "that ain't really fair, you know, considering you ain't ever seen Miss Blythe drive. She handles the ribbons a fair treat, she does. For a female."

Dalton turned his withering gaze upon his tiger. "I think you'd do well to keep out of this, Jack. I'll deal with you later for your part in this night's fiasco."

"I just thought you ought to know that this 'ere scratch weren't Miss Blythe's fault." Jack stuck stubbornly to his guns. "Some nob in 'is cups swerved right into 'er. I doubt if you yourself could 'ave dodged 'im."

His lordship's look was a scornful contradiction, but Jenny was touched. "Why, thank you, Jack," she said warmly. "And, remember what I said about employment. You could grow to like Birmingham."

"Oh? So, Miss Blythe, you aren't content just to

steal my equipage. You plan to steal my tiger as well?"

"Only if you're sapskull enough to discharge him. Now if your lordship will excuse me, it's been a very trying evening." She began to climb down from the box. He put up a hand, reluctantly, to help her.

She winced as she surveyed the ugly scar on the pristine newness of his coach body. "Send me the bill for that, Lord Dalton."

"Damn the bill. It's your blasted effrontery that I'm incensed over. I realize that for some unfathomable reason, my rigs hold a great fascination for you. But why you had to pick this particular time to prove your prowess as a whip is beyond me. Do you have any idea of how next to impossible it is to secure a hackney once Astley's has let out?"

Jenny ignored the question. She was chewing over a part of the preamble to it. "Proving my prowess as a whip?" She glared. "Did you truly think that was what this was all about?"

"God knows what this was all about. A pleasure jaunt, perhaps?"

" 'A pleasure jaunt'! Well, that really is the outside of enough," she said wearily, all the starch suddenly draining out of her. "I know you don't think very highly of me, Lord Dalton, but I did think you'd realize that I would never have taken your rig so—cavalierly—if it hadn't been an emergency."

"Then suppose you tell me about it." He was studying her face and his tone had softened.

"Really, I'd rather not."

"Come, Miss Blythe. I do think you owe me that much. And whatever it is, I can assure you, I'm not a gabble-grinder."

She hesitated a moment longer and then capitulated. "Oh, very well then. You probably know all about this already, judging from the mischief-making hints your friends have dropped. The thing is, you see, Claire saw her father at the circus tonight with two small children. And"—Jenny swallowed—"she wanted to follow and see where they went. We couldn't get a hackney, either. And she was frantic, so . . ." She gestured eloquently toward his coach.

"Oh, my God. You drove all the way to Covent Garden with just him?" He nodded toward Jack, who looked offended.

"So you do know."

"Yes, and I wish you'd come to get me. I could have taken you or, better still, saved you the trip. For I'm afraid it's common knowledge that Lord Hazlett keeps a mistress and that they have two children. I am sorry that Lady Claire had to discover it. She's bound to be upset." He grimaced at his understatement.

"She's devastated. Now I really must go see about her. And I truly am sorry for all the inconveniences I've caused you. And I will pay for the damage. I insist."

"No, you'll do nothing of the kind." Lord Dalton smiled a twisted smile. "I'd far liefer hold a grudge. If you and I should ever sheathe our daggers, I'd feel totally at a loss. Good night, Miss Blythe." To her surprise he reached for her gloved hand and brought it lightly to his lips. "Go drink a tisane. If you don't get a case of the grippe from all this exposure, it will be a miracle."

He watched her inside and remained staring

thoughtfully at the front door for several seconds after it had closed.

Jack watched him watch. The tiger's eyes were bright with interest.

Sylvia was waiting in Jenny's bedchamber. She was in her nightclothes, settled on the couch with a candle on the stand beside her and a book in her hand that she'd been quite unable to read. She jumped up when Jenny entered.

"Where have you been?" she demanded in a whisper. "I've been beside myself with worry."

"I am sorry." Jenny shed her cloak and came over to sit wearily beside her cousin. Oh, dear, she thought, I can't possibly go through all this again. I'm far too tired. But she knew that she owed an explanation to Sylvia for the anxious evening she'd spent.

Sylvia listened intently without interruption, her face mirroring her compassion for her cousin Claire. Then she sat silently for a bit, lost in thought, and when she spoke her voice was bitter. "He knew it all along," she said.

"Lord Dalton? Why, yes, he did."

She shook her head impatiently. "No, not Dalton. Mr. Chalgrove. He knew all along that our uncle has another family. And he tried to fling it in Claire's teeth. That was—cruel."

She jumped up suddenly and hurried from the room.

Jenny undressed and crawled wearily into bed, where the events of the evening whirled in her brain like so many speeding horses in the ring at Astley's Circus. And just before she finally fell asleep she suddenly recalled Sylvia's odd reaction.

Mr. Chalgrove indeed! It was beyond her just what Mr. Chalgrove had to say to anything. Still, maybe it was true that every cloud has its silver lining. If this miserable evening had made the scales fall from Sylvia's eyes and she now saw that odious coxcomb clearly, at least that was one small outcome to the good.

Chapter Seventeen

ANOTHER FORTUNATE CIRCUMSTANCE, as Jenny discovered the following day, was that neither Fremantle nor his stepmama was aware that the cousins had not come home together the night before. Her ladyship had been invited to dinner, followed by cards, and Lord Fremantle had spent a rare evening at his club. Jenny breathed a prayer of thanksgiving for this deliverance as she went in search of Claire.

She found her cousin at the pianoforte, lightly strumming the keys. "Are you all right?" she asked.

"Certainly," was the bland reply. "Why shouldn't I be?" She stopped playing to dig a chocolate out of her pocket and pop it into her mouth.

Jenny tried, none too successfully, to keep the concern out of her voice. "There's no reason not to be, actually. But last night you did seem upset, so I was worried."

"Well, it was a shock," Claire admitted, "but now I've had time to accustom myself to the idea. And really"—she began to play again—"there's nothing at all unusual in the situation. I expect that most gentlemen, if the truth be known, have their love nests. That is the proper term, is it not?"

"Well, it's certainly one of them," Jenny said dryly.

"Why, just look at the Regent. He's certainly never lacked for mistresses. Though if he's had any out-of-wedlock children, I've not heard of it. But the royal dukes have."

"Well, the Duke of Clarence, certainly."

"So it was silly of me to make so much of the situation. And I'm sorry to have put you through all that last night. Was Lord Dalton furious?"

"No, not really. At least not for long."

"So all's well that ends well." Claire spoke a bit too heartily, but Jenny inwardly applauded the effort. "So now let's just forget about it, shall we?"

"Consider it forgotten."

Jenny left Claire to her playing and went off to write an expurgated version of her London adventures to her family and then to settle in for a long session with a Gothic novel. Just as she'd reached the climax and a chain-clanking specter was set to do its worst, she was interrupted by a very young and nervous maid who announced that her ladyship was ready to receive callers and expected her nieces to join her. "I've informed Lady Sylvia, miss, but I can't find Lady Claire anywhere."

"Oh?" Jenny reluctantly closed her book. "Have you tried the drawing room?"

"Yes, miss. And she's not at the pianoforte."

"Well, never mind. I'll find her."

Some sixth sense was making Jenny quite uneasy. The unease grew when she checked Claire's wardrobe and found that her cloak was missing. As she emerged from her cousin's chamber, the maid was just coming to find her. "Oh, miss"—the girl's eyes were saucerlike—"Edward the footman just told me he saw Lady Claire go out by herself and flag down a hackney coach, cool as ever you please."

"Oh, my word." Jenny thought swiftly. "Listen, Jill, if she asks, you must tell my aunt that Lady Claire and I have gone to the circulating library and will be back shortly."

"Oh, but miss—"

"Just do it!" Jenny snapped, and ran to snatch her own cloak and reticule.

She thought it best to take the servants' stairs and emerged onto the street from the lower level. How Claire had managed to find a hackney so easily was more than she could imagine. Now there was not one in sight. Lord Dalton's phaeton was standing in front of Fremantle House, however. Jack had momentarily abandoned his post to wheedle a cup of tea from the kitchen.

"Oh, why not," Jenny muttered to herself, and sprinted toward the rig. At that instant Jack emerged, tea in hand. But the fact that he froze in horror gave her the advantage. She was established in the driver's seat before he reacted. He did not give up easily, however. Tea splashing from the cup, he chased her down the street, whooping, "Oh, no, please! Not again! Do come back, miss! 'is Lordship'll skin me alive this time for sure."

"I'm sorry, Jack," she called. "Just tell Lord Dalton I'll be right back. I've gone to fetch my cousin."

At the entrance to Russel Street Claire paid off her driver and walked slowly down it. She earned a few curious glances; such a well-dressed young lady, all alone, was obviously out of place here. She hesitated in front of the house that her father had entered the night before. It was a modest, unpretentious dwelling, but from the newly painted shutters to the tiny, well-tended patch of garden, a lot of care had been lovingly lavished upon it.

Claire almost lost her courage. Indeed had she told the hackney driver to wait (her first inclination), she would have fled. She now toyed with the idea of returning to a main thoroughfare in hopes of finding another. Such a course of action seemed craven, though. She had come this far. She squared her shoulders and started up the gravel walk.

Since the woman who answered the door was drying her hands on the apron she wore, Claire took it for granted she was a servant of some sort. She was a pleasant-looking female of young middle age, with a round face under her crisp white cap. Very bright, very blue large eyes were her only claim to beauty. She gave Claire a cordial, if somewhat puzzled, smile.

For the first time it occurred to Claire that she hadn't the faintest notion whom to ask for. The sound of children's voices in the background did little to calm her agitation.

"Might I—I see your mistress?" she stammered.

The woman laughed at that. "Lord save us, I'm the only one that's here. Maid and mistress all in one packet you could say. I think perhaps you're at the wrong house, m'dear."

"No, I don't believe so. I'm Lord Hazlett's daughter."

The woman looked as if she'd just been struck. But she quickly rallied and said quietly, "You'll want to come in then, won't you?"

She ushered Claire into a tiny parlor, made to appear even smaller by the profusion of toys littering every surface. A cozy fire burned in the fireplace. There were bookcases on each side of it, filled with well-thumbed volumes. The chairs and sofa were worn, but comfortable. Underneath all the clutter of blocks and dolls and balls and soldiers the place was shiny clean. And despite that clutter, or perhaps because of it, the small room seemed inviting. Claire could not prevent herself from comparing it with the spacious elegance of her own house. It was hard to imagine the lord of that manor here in this humble setting. She thought it better not to try.

"Let me fetch some tea."

"Oh, no, please," Claire said, now wishing she had never invaded this woman's privacy, hating herself for the distress she must be causing. "You shouldn't go to any trouble on my account."

"Oh, it's no trouble at all, Lady Claire. It will only take a moment." She lifted a toy donkey cart off a wing chair and indicated that Claire should sit there. "Do excuse the mess." She looked helplessly around her, a proud housewife caught in an awkward moment. "I tell Hazlett that it's sinful to have so many toys, but he will keep bringing them." Her cheeks flamed at what she'd just said and she hurried from the room.

Claire sat with folded hands, staring at the fire, resisting the urge to bolt. She hadn't thought beyond her own need to come here. Now how was she to explain such an unforgivable action? It somehow made it all seem worse that the mistress of the house knew her name.

It very slowly penetrated her consciousness that the babble of childish voices she'd first heard upon entering had stopped. Claire looked around to see two pairs of enormous eyes staring at her.

They stood in the doorway, the two tots from the circus. The little boy was about four, she judged, and his sister couldn't be older than two. Her thumb was planted firmly in her mouth as she regarded the newcomer solemnly.

"Gwenny's afraid of strangers," the little boy announced.

"But you're not, are you?"

"Of course not," was the scornful answer.

"And what's your name?"

"Will." He was inching closer, his sister following.

Will for William. He had her father's name.

When their mother returned a few moments later carrying a tray laden with a teapot, cups, and assorted biscuits, Claire was seated on the floor with the two children, helping to construct a castle of the blocks. "I saw my father and the children at Astley's Circus," she explained in a rush. "And I had to see them. I somehow knew, you see, though no one told me. And—well, I've always longed for brothers and sisters. My cousin Jenny is oldest of an enormous brood, and I did so envy her. Your children are adorable Mrs.— Oh, dear," she broke off in consternation. "I don't even know your name."

"It's Mrs. Rogers." She carefully placed the tea tray on the worn carpet next to Claire and sat down beside it. "I was a widow when I met your father— Now stop it, Will," she broke off as Gwenny demolished the castle, and William let out a roar. "Don't hit your little sister."

"Never mind, we'll build it back," Claire interposed diplomatically, and quickly began stacking blocks.

As Will became absorbed once more in the project, she said in a low voice, "He looks so very much like Father."

Mrs. Rogers brightened. "Oh, do you think so? So do I, but Hazlett pooh-poohs the notion."

"He's just being modest. I know how he's always longed for a son. And it was easy to tell, even at the circus, that he dotes on little Gwenny." Claire tried hard to keep any traces of jealousy from her voice.

"Well, men always dote on their daughters, don't they, dear? They may say they want sons, but it's the daughters who twist their heartstrings. You should hear him rave on and on about you."

"About me?" Claire tried to force a smile and failed. "I'm afraid you exaggerate, Mrs. Rogers. There's nothing about me to rave about."

"Well, if that's so, no one's told Hazlett," Mrs. Rogers replied firmly. "He never tires of talking about how talented you are. A regular prodigy you were, to hear him tell it. Oh, there's nothing like the firstborn, you know. No other child can ever quite measure up. I know that from my own family. The sun rose and set in my oldest brother. But I am hoping that little Gwenny may have a bit of your musical ability. She does sing along with her papa already," she said proudly, "though of course it's early days to really tell if there's talent there. She can never hope to be the beauty you are, though. Looks too much like me for that, I fear."

"Thank goodness she doesn't look like me. I wouldn't wish that on her."

Mrs. Rogers gazed at Claire in astonishment. "Why, I do believe you're serious. Don't you know what a nonpareil you are?"

136

"That's ridiculous. What I am is . . . fat."

"Well . . ." Mrs. Rogers looked her over judiciously. "You certainly aren't one of the skin-and-bones type—which gentlemen don't care for all that much in my experience. And everything else about you is perfection—your hair, your eyes, your complexion. Surely you must know that."

"Well," Claire said doubtfully, "I think I probably have lost a bit of weight just lately. My aunt has had me on a special diet, you see." She chuckled suddenly and told Mrs. Rogers how Lord Fremantle had had her meals smuggled to her room.

Mrs. Rogers laughed and clapped her hands. "Oh, your cousin sounds like such a nice gentleman."

"Oh, yes, indeed, he certainly is," Claire responded enthusiastically.

The gentleman in question had returned to his house a bit before to find Lord Dalton on his doorstep dressing down his tiger. Lord Fremantle handed the reins of his curricle to his own servant and went to see what the altercation was all about. At the same moment the front door opened and the butler joined the group.

"Is there a problem, Dalton?" his lordship inquired politely.

"Not really." Dalton sighed. "It's just that this mutton-headed lad of mine has developed the habit of allowing my rigs to be taken out from underneath his nose. But I beg pardon, Fremantle. I shouldn't have chosen your front doorway to strip the young rascal's hide off."

Fremantle looked horrified. "My word! You mean that your phaeton's been stolen?"

"Not stolen—borrowed."

On the step above, Jackson cleared his throat. "I think, m'lord—at least Edward tells me—that Lady Claire departed in a hackney coach a bit ago and now Miss Jenny has—err—*borrowed* His Lordship's carriage to go fetch her."

"How . . . odd!" Lord Fremantle was not given to hyperbole. His face, however, reflected his astonishment.

"I think I've a very good notion of where they're off to," Dalton said grimly.

"You have?" Fremantle turned to the butler. "No need for you to catch your death out here in the cold, Jackson." His tone was dismissive.

As soon as the reluctant butler was out of earshot, Dalton quickly filled Fremantle in on the details of the night before. "I don't doubt for a minute that Jenny believes her cousin's gone to Russel Street," he finished. It was an indication of both states of mind that neither gentleman noticed his free use of Miss Blythe's name. "If you'll lend me your rig, I'll go fetch them."

"I think that's more my responsibility."

"Of course," Dalton said hastily. "But you won't object if I come along? I have a vested interest. In my rig, that is. Besides, my poor excuse for a tiger knows the exact direction."

They were proceeding down Old Bond Street at a pace that Lord Fremantle considered a rapid clip and Lord Dalton found so sedate that it set his teeth on edge when they became aware of an altercation up head.

"Oh, my prophetic soul!" was Dalton's Shakespearean reaction.

"Lor' save us; she's struck again!" Jack offered more prosaically.

The Piccadilly intersection had become a tangle of carts, carriages, and cursing, shouting passengers and drivers. Above it all, tall and stately on the box of the high-perch phaeton, sat Miss Jenny Blythe, the haughty target for most of the invective that dinned the air.

Lord Fremantle pulled his horses to a halt, and Lord Dalton leaped down from the passenger seat onto the pavement. "You go on, Fremantle. I'll tend to this," he called over his shoulder. "Stay with his lordship, Jack. He'll need you to locate the house for him."

There must have been something about the cut of Dalton's five-caped greatcoat, the tilt of his curly beaver over his brow, his gleaming boots, his soft leather gloves, the cane he carried, but most of all, the expression on his aristocratic face that bespoke authority. At any rate the crowd parted before him like Red Sea rushes. He halted by the step of his property and gazed up into the face of his nemesis.

"How now, Miss Blythe?" he queried.

Chapter Eighteen

At first, Lady Fremantle was not particularly displeased that two of her nieces weren't present to help her receive visitors. She had more or less washed her hands of the Honorable Jenny and Lady Claire. Their lack of social success was more than compensated for by Sylvia's.

Lady Fremantle looked with satisfaction at her favorite niece, now surrounded with a bevy of admirers. She was, indeed, a pretty child. And modest with it. Even the most censorious of Lady Fremantle's friends could find no fault with Sylvia. The come-out had been a success after all. Oh, not the triumph of twenty years ago, of course, but her ladyship could not, in all honesty, wish for that.

"Mr. Chalgrove seems most reluctant to leave," a friend remarked as she rose to go. "I'm sure he was here before I was."

"He's probably waiting to speak with Lord Dalton." Lady Fremantle looked smug. "His lordship visits us every day now. And he and Chalgrove are particular friends, you know."

Chalgrove was not waiting for Dalton. What he wished was a private word with Lady Sylvia. He seized his opportunity when the gentlemen surrounding her rose and took their leave of Lady Fremantle.

"Is there something wrong?" He inched his chair closer and spoke in a low voice.

Her glare took him aback. He would not have dreamed that Sylvia was capable of such hostility. "My cousin Claire knows everything now. I do hope her misery makes you happy, Mr. Chalgrove."

He turned quite pale. "I've no notion of what you're talking about," he protested.

"Oh, have you not?" Her lip curled with scorn. "You were dropping hints about her father's other family right here at our own ball. Can you deny it?"

"No," he replied. None of Chalgrove's acquaintances would have believed he could look so stricken. "But at the time I—"

"I should have listened when they told me what you were like," she interrupted, her low voice bitter. "They said you actually enjoy exposing other people's scandals for the unfeeling to snicker over. But I could not believe it of you till I heard of my uncle's situation and then remembered what you'd said. Well, enjoy your little laugh, Mr. Chalgrove. And if anything of that nature ever happens to me, at least I'll know that *someone* gets pleasure from my humiliation. Now I think you'd better go. And I should prefer not to see you again, Mr. Chalgrove."

Chalgrove brushed past the butler, who had hastily leaped to open the outer door at the sight of his face. "The devil take her," he muttered between clenched teeth as he made his way, with angry strides, toward his club. Who would have thought that sweet, gentle Sylvia could turn on one like

141

that? Her eyes had actually snapped, he now recalled. "Dalton's in for a rude surprise," he said,
chuckling bitterly. "He'll think he's captured an
angel for himself; instead he'll get a shrew."

Mr. Chalgrove slowed his steps. He suddenly realized he did not wish to go to White's after all. For
he was not sure just how long he could nurse this
anger he was feeling. And instinct told him that
once he'd let it go, he was due for the worst fit of
the dismals of his life.

Lady Claire had proceeded on foot a little way
down Russel Street when Lord Fremantle's carriage pulled up beside her. She gaped in astonishment.

"How did you know?" she asked as he handed
her up.

"That's rather an odd story. Can it wait just a
bit?" He clucked at his horses.

"I collect you need to give me a scold first," she
sighed.

"Well, yes, as a matter of fact, I must," he replied
gently. "Cousin Claire, it's not at all the thing for
you to go traipsing around London alone. Particularly in this part of town. Why did you not tell me
that you needed to come here? I would have brought
you."

She looked up at him in wonderment. "You would
actually do that? I didn't suppose that you'd approve."

"My approving or not approving has nothing to
say in the matter. If you felt you needed to come
here, then I would have brought you," he answered
simply.

"Oh, cousin, you are so kind." Her eyes filled with
142

tears. She impulsively laid a hand upon his sleeve, then quickly removed it.

They rode a moment in silence. Claire realized she was feeling a wonderful sense of peace. How much of it was due to her recent visit and how much to the solid presence beside her wasn't a ratio she could sort out. "You knew about my father's—other family—didn't you?"

He looked uncomfortable. "Well, yes. I had heard about the liaison."

"Can you understand that I just had to see for myself?"

"No, I really can't," he replied seriously. "You see, I can scarcely remember my own father, so I've no notion of what such a revelation would be like."

"Well, at first it was a terrible shock," she admitted candidly. "Rather like being kicked in the stomach, I collect. And I felt betrayed. I confess I was really bitter at my father."

"I should think that would be a perfectly normal reaction."

"But then, over and above everything else, I kept thinking, I have a little half-brother and sister that I've never met. And that seemed—intolerable.

"And, oh, Cousin James, they are the most cunning children. Little Will is so bright—and bossy. But the baby refuses to be bear-led. We actually played together on the floor. And it was delightful. I do wish"—her face grew wistful—"that they were truly my brother and sister. I hated being an only child, you see."

"Yes, I can understand that."

"Of course you can." She smiled up at him. "But do you know," she went on seriously, "what has

143

been the strangest thing of all? I actually liked Mrs. Rogers."

"Did you indeed?" His voice was noncommittal, his eyes fastened on the road.

"Yes, I did. And I was quite prepared to hold her in contempt. That sort of woman. You know the terms you hear. Light-skirt. Cyprian. But she's nothing at all like that. She's nice and soft-spoken and a very good mother. And—well, it's obvious that she loves my father. But do you know what the strangest thing is about her?"

"No, what?" He guided his team carefully around a farmer's cart loaded with straw.

"She's plain. No, *plain* is not the right word at all, for she has the kindest face—that really lights up when she smiles, eyes and all. But she really has no claim in the least to beauty. She's not terribly young now, of course, but I can't believe she ever could have done."

"Well, is that so very strange, my dear?" Lord Fremantle looked puzzled. "Most of the world's population falls into that category. Otherwise your family would not have created the sensation that it did."

"I realize that. But I should have thought a—mistress"—she choked a bit over the word—"would have to be ravishing. In order to pull a man away from his wife and family, I mean. Especially—" She left the words unsaid.

"When the wife is a celebrated beauty?" he supplied. "Well, I'm certainly no authority on the subject, but there are other qualities besides beauty that cause a man to fall in love."

"I was always taught that it was the only thing worth having for a female."

144

"I know you were."

"But I also know my parents were never happy. They quarreled incessantly when I was small. And then Papa began to stay away longer and longer. That's why I dreaded this come-out so much," she blurted out. "I know everyone thinks of the Percival sisters as Cinderellas. But in my mama's case, it doesn't fit at all. Or perhaps," she said reflectively, "Mama did get what she wanted out of life. Papa's very wealthy, you know. Perhaps he was the only one disappointed. And I should be glad, I collect, that now he has found happiness."

"Oh, should you indeed, Claire?" He smiled down at her. "You don't think that's carrying Christian forebearance too far, then?"

She'd never known her serious cousin to tease before and she giggled in response. "I did sound dreadfully sanctimonious, didn't I? All right then. I'm not *glad*, exactly. But I can truly say that I'm no longer bitter."

"And that's quite good enough," he pronounced firmly. "I'd rather hate it if you were suddenly elevated to sainthood."

"Well, I am mostly pleased about the children. Though I'll go ahead and admit to being a little jealous as well, since you seem to see right through my hypocrisy. For I can't help but envy their relationship with my father. He used to be my father, too, you see."

"Claire," Fremantle said earnestly, "you mustn't make too much of the fact that your father hasn't been to see you since you've been in London. I think he was merely trying to save you embarrassment. He is the object of a great deal of gossip, of course."

"That *could* be the reason." She sounded doubtful. "And I wonder if my mother really believes he's out of the country. Do you suppose she knows the situation?"

"Well, it would amaze me if someone hasn't informed her by now," he answered dryly. He didn't add that his stepmama would be a prime candidate. "That could explain why she didn't wish to come to London."

"In part, perhaps." She did not sound convinced. "Of course, Mama could have written Papa to stay away during my come-out," she mused. By the by, I asked Mrs. Rogers not to tell him I'd visited. It would only upset him, I'm sure."

"That was wise of you, Claire. And considerate."

"Do you know that Mrs. Rogers says he talks of me constantly? And that he's—proud of me?"

"That's hardly amazing."

"Of course, she might have made it up. I told you that she's kind."

"That will do, Claire!" He frowned down at her. "I do, as a rule, despise conceit. But, damme, the other extreme is equally bad—or worse. Your father has every reason to be proud of you. You are not only extremely talented, you have a lovely character. And though I confess I'm glad that you don't seem to prize it, you must surely know that you are beautiful."

Her eyes widened in amazement. "That's what Mrs. Rogers said."

"Blast Mrs. Rogers! It's what *I* say."

Lord Fremantle actually whipped up his team.

Chapter Nineteen

JENNY WAS NOT about to admit even to herself just how glad she was to see Lord Dalton. She watched, with respect mingled with resentment, as he dispersed the crowd.

"Well, I could have done that, too, with a full purse," she observed acidly as he climbed up on the driver's side and picked up the reins. "Don't you think bribery is rather contemptible?"

"Would you rather they mobbed you?"

"They wouldn't do that."

"Maybe not. But there was talk of fetching the Runners."

"I wish they had done. Then I might have explained that none of this was my fault."

"That's not what the cart owner says. He says you came flying into the crossing, which caused his animal to rear and upset his cart."

"Fustian. And your paying him off as tantamount to admitting my guilt."

"Exactly."

"You really are an odious man, you know." She made the observation with scientific detachment as she gazed at his classic profile.

"Not at all. In fact, I'm amazed at the forebearance I'm developing. My foes won't even recognize me, I've become so mellowed."

"What are you doing?" she asked as he turned right onto St. Martin's Lane. "I thought you knew I was going to Covent Garden. It's that way." She pointed back over her shoulder.

"Thank you for that guide to my city," he said sarcastically. "Fremantle's fetching your cousin. I don't think it requires a regiment."

"No, I was quite prepared to do it myself."

"And a right proper mess you were making of it, too."

"That was not my fault, as I've been— Why are we stopping here?" she asked as he pulled his horses over.

"Well, Miss Blythe, if you are going to make it a habit to help yourself to my rigs at will, I think it's high time you learned to drive. And I, God help me, am about to teach you."

"I'm not planning to ever touch one of your precious carriages again. Nor would I have done so today except that it was the first thing to hand."

"Bit of luck then, I'd say, that His Royal Highness didn't happen to be calling."

"Besides, I know how to drive."

"So you've demonstrated. Now quit arguing and climb over me before I change my mind."

She did actually follow his instructions. It was due entirely to the circumstance that one of the horses decided to step forward that she landed in his lap.

"Clumsy," he muttered, extracting the ostrich feather that adorned her bonnet from his mouth.

"Can I help it if you don't hold your horses?"

The seat exchange and reins transfer having been

accomplished, "Now let's see you crack that whip," his lordship ordered.

"There hardly seems any necessity for that. You surely can't wish me to spring 'em."

"What I wish to do— No, correct that. What I *feel compelled* to do is to teach you to drive this rig. And in the event you need to employ that whip you'd better learn how."

"Do you have to sit so close?" she asked crossly.

"Yes. I have considerable affection for my team. I want to be in a position to rescue them."

"Well, give me room to operate." She plucked the whip from its holder.

He obligingly scooted over a few inches. His eyes were fixed critically upon her.

The long whip snaked and cracked. The look she shot him was smugly satisfied.

"Watch out!" he shouted, lunging to snatch the reins and steer the team out of the path of an oncoming coach. "Watch where you're going!" he snarled, as Miss Blythe's face flamed red at the expletive hurled their way by the irate coachman.

"Well, what do you expect," she snapped back, "with you telling me what to do? I *said* it was folly to crack the whip."

"The only folly involved was your looking for my approval instead of watching the street."

"You must admit I handled the whip well."

"It was . . . all right."

" 'All right'?" She glared at him indignantly, and his gloved hands landed once more atop hers on the reins.

"That's really not at all necessary." The truth was, his proximity, as always, was most unsettling.

149

Whether she found it more irritating than pleasurable was best left unexplored.

They drove in silence for a bit, Jenny doing her best to concentrate. "By the by, where are we going?" she finally inquired.

"We'll drive down the Strand," he replied, with martyred resignation. "You might as well experience the thick of traffic."

She could have managed quite nicely without him. It wasn't the other vehicles crowding the thoroughfare that presented a problem. It was knowing that his confidence in her ability was nil, that he sat tense and ready to take over at any given moment. They had proceeded up the Strand for some little distance without incident, Jenny stopping and starting her team as the necessity arose and with considerable aplomb, or so she thought. She was on the verge of saying that he surely could relax now, when he suddenly froze beside her. "Oh, dear God," he breathed.

"Now really! There's no need for that. You're making an absolute nervous wreck of me." She glared up at him to discover that his attention was not on her at all. His gaze was riveted on the upper reaches of a tall mercantile establishment. She followed the direction of it and her blood ran cold. "Oh, dear God!" she echoed.

From a five-storey height, the building dominated its row. It was a handsome edifice, built of ancient brick. An arched entryway was a full storey tall, flanked by demicolumns and surmounted by the company's coat of arms, executed in marble, taking up the full height of another storey. Not content with that much adornment, the architect had continued upward with more marble, more half columns, this time framing windows and forming niches for classical statuary. And above it all, at a dizzying height, there stood the stone figure of a goddess upon a marble ledge. A marble arch curved gracefully behind her at shoulder height, sloping down to culminate in two short ledges, a continuation of the one the goddess stood on. Behind her, with an oeil-de-boeuf for balance on each side, was a large, open, arched window. A small tot had just crawled out it and was peering delightedly around the goddess's head.

Dalton leaped from the high-perch phaeton and sprinted across the street, oblivious to the traffic.

"Hey, you! You, there!" Jenny screeched at a crossing sweep who was pushing his broom idly back and forth. "Come hold these horses."

The lad was quick to respond, motivated as much by the elegance of her equipage as the urgency in her voice. "Pay you when I get back," she said, and began to run after his lordship.

"Cor!" the street urchin breathed as he located the source of Jenny's panic. In the short interval of time it had taken to engage the sweep, the tot had decided to explore further. He was settled on his small posterior now and, making delighted gurgling noises, was scooting his way down the marble arch.

Jenny, her pelisse hiked up to a scandalous altitude, took the steps of the staircase two at a time. She arrived panting to see Lord Dalton, who had already shed both his coats, pull off his Hessians.

"Oh, do be careful," she breathed as he stepped up upon the windowsill.

She had not expected an answer, of course, but she noted with an increase of alarm that his lordship appeared incapable of making one. He was every bit as white as the polished marble. He stood statuelike, a rival to the goddess, for just one second, then he climbed out the window and, with a death grip upon the sill, lowered himself onto the ledge.

The toddler had suddenly become aware of his predicament and was giving tongue. The howls did little for his lordship's equilibrium. They did, however, alert the youngster's mother to his disappearance. She came popping out a closed door, into the hallway, and looked frantically around. "Earnest, where are you?" she called. For answer there was an increase in the volume of the howls coming from outside.

Jenny pulled her head in to deal with this new development. "It's all right. His lordship will fetch him," she said soothingly as she tried to prevent the young mother from looking out. In this she was completely unsuccessful. The woman did lean out, did look, and went into strong hysterics. Jenny jerked her away from the sill and administered a sharp slap.

It was effective. The woman collapsed upon the floor, rocking back and forth with near-silent sobs. "Sorry," Jenny muttered. "But your caterwauling will send them both—" She choked on the sentence and leaned out the window once again.

His lordship, she saw, had reached the child and was now speaking soothingly to him. Jenny held her breath as he carefully eased himself down to a sitting position, his legs dangling off into space. "What's your name, lad?" he asked conversationally.

"E'nest," was the choked reply.

"Well, Earnest, I'm going to carry you back up

152

to the window. But you're going to have to help. You must hold on tight and not wiggle. Think you can manage that?" The child nodded. "All right, then. Here goes."

Slowly, carefully, Dalton lifted the youngster while Jenny ceased to breathe. Earnest's little arms came together around his lordship's neck in a stranglehold. "Not quite so tight, boy," he managed to croak.

Oh, please, God, Jenny prayed silently, as, pressing his back against the wall, Dalton struggled slowly to his feet. One arm clasped the child; the other hand pressed against the brick for purchase. It seemed to take forever, but at last he stood. Stood and swayed sufficiently to send up a concerted gasp from the crowd of spectators that had spied the elevated drama and were huddled, necks craned, below.

People were gathering inside as well. A gentleman from the office she'd just vacated was ministering to the stricken mother. Others tried to crowd round Jenny at the window till she told them in no uncertain terms for God's sake to stand back.

Slowly, slowly, slowly, Lord Dalton inched his stocking feet across the narrow marble ledge, pressing back against the arch as he did so. Jenny, leaning far out the window to her own peril, strung together soft words of encouragement. "Fine. Good. Famous. You're doing great. Just don't look down. You're almost there. About three more steps now and you can reach the statue."

The three steps seemed to take three hours to her way of thinking. But at last he was there, beneath the window. "Can you peel the little beggar off me?" he managed to gasp.

153

"I think so." She leaned out even further. "But your hand's in my way. Move it off the wall and brace against the statue.

She waited for him to comply. Nothing happened. "Dalton!"

"I . . . don't think I can do that," came the muffled reply.

"Do it! Now!" Jenny employed the same tone she'd used with the hysterical mother.

The wet palm left the marble and grabbed the goddess's shoulder in a vise.

Earnest didn't want to leave the secure shoulder he was plastered on. As Jenny grabbed his arms she used all the persuasion at her command to make him turn loose the two handfuls of cambric that he clutched. Dalton seemed to have nothing to say in the matter. With closed eyes, he was clinging to the marble goddess.

The tot's mother, however, managed to rise to the occasion. She appeared in the window beside Jenny. "Do what the nice lady says, Earnest," she wheedled. And with a howl that sent the pigeons flying, the child suddenly turned loose. He did, but not Dalton.

"Let the boy loose," Jenny hissed. And as he obediently released his hold on Earnest to transfer that hand to the marble arch, she plucked the screaming child inside.

Earnest was placed in his mother's arms—who now felt free to reindulge in her hysterics. The other people rallied around to comfort and congratulate, leaving Jenny alone to focus her attention upon Lord Dalton.

"You can come in now," she told him.

"I . . . don't . . . think . . . so," he replied.

"Of course you can," she said heartily. "The bad part's over. You can't possibly take a tumble. The statue's a buffer. Come on now."

"Sorry. Can't move," he mumbled.

Oh, dear God; he really is frozen there, she realized. Once more to her peril Jenny leaned far out to pat his head reassuringly. "Come on. Just one more effort, Dalton. You can do it. I won't let you fall."

"That's about as damned silly a statement as I've ever heard."

She giggled. In spite of every circumstance, Jenny giggled. It occurred to her that she might be no better in a crisis than Earnest's mother. "You're right, you know," she managed to tell him. "But do turn around and get yourself back in here. I don't know about you, but I really need a cup of tea."

Her matter-of-fact tone evidently did the trick. He began to rotate slowly while the spectators held their breaths. He completed the rotation by embracing the stone goddess like a lover. He shinnied halfway up her, then, with his legs locked tightly around her, reached out to grasp the window ledge. Dalton heaved himself up and over, whereupon he slid down onto the floor and put his head between his knees.

It took some persuasion on Jenny's part to prevail upon the knot of people to go away and leave them alone. Earnest's mother was profuse in her thanks, kneeling down at his lordship's level, still sobbing intermittently. As she poured out her gratitude, she kept a tight grip on Earnest, who was now struggling to get out of her arms. The only response from Lord Dalton was a dismissing wave of the hand.

"Please, leave him alone," Jenny asked. "And, no, I'd best not tell you his name. He's extremely modest, you see, and hates having a fuss made over him."

"If you say so." Earnest's mother's tone was frosty. She had obviously not forgiven the slap. She rose to her feet, however, though she appeared to feel that something was lacking. The look she gave the prostrated Dalton was clearly dissatisfied.

After Jenny explained that she felt quite faint and wished to just sit quietly a moment and regain her equilibrium, the people ringed above her and Dalton did at last disperse. She turned then to his lordship, whose head still rested on his knees. "I think that was the bravest thing I've ever seen," she said.

He did raise his head then to stare straight at her. It was the mother of all baleful looks. "You're really enjoying this, aren't you?"

"Of course not!" She was indignant. Then native honesty took over. "Well, I collect I am rather pleased to discover that you're human after all."

" 'Human'!" The look actually increased its intensity. "Why not go ahead and say it. When it comes to heights, I'm a quivering jelly." His head now rested back against the wall. "Always have been."

"Oh, that was perfectly obvious from the very first. That was what made your action so heroic."

" 'Heroic'!" His lip curled.

"Exactly. I meant what I said, even if you don't believe me. I thought that forcing yourself out on that narrow ledge when you obviously couldn't bear to do so was really brave. And did you notice that as long as Earnest's welfare was uppermost in your

156

mind you were all right? It was only when you'd turned him safely over to me that you—err—fell apart."

" 'Fell apart.' You do have a way with words, Miss Blythe, that goes a long way to restore a cove's manhood. Dammit," he said musingly, "why did that blasted brat have to choose the one way to imperil his life that would totally unnerve me? He might just as easily have tumbled off Westminster Bridge. I swim like a fish, you know."

"Yes, but have you thought of the height of that selfsame bridge?" She tried to keep a straight face, then snickered.

"Damn you," he said pleasantly. "Actually, that would have been no problem. After I'd gotten sick and dizzy on the ledge and *fallen* in the water, I'd have gotten us both out with ease."

"Yes, I can see that. And how are you with burning buildings?"

"Oh, first rate."

"I can picture you now, dashing through a wall of flames."

"Why do I feel that you'll never let me hear the end of this?"

"Because you're a silly ass," she replied seriously. "I've more respect for you now than I would have dreamed possible. Oh, I've heard all those stories of what a Nonesuch you are. A fearless pugilist. A champion cricket player. A neck-or-nothing rider. York-Jones raves on ad nauseum. But to make yourself do something that's so against the grain. That's *really* bravery. Whereas getting knocked around by Gentleman Jackson in the ring is merely stupid."

"Thank you for that analogy. What I should have

done, of course, was step aside and let you pull Master Earnest off the ledge."

"You think I could have done so?"

"In a tick. No doubt about it. You'd have probably skipped along the ledge, la-de-dah, la-de-dah," he finished bitterly.

She sighed. "I do tend to give that impression, don't I? It's a kind of curse. Comes along with my height. It's silly to even try to appear fragile and fluttery, given my size. But as for what you just said, no, I don't think I could have done what you did. If there was no one around more capable, I'd like to think I would have tried. But I doubt that I could have gotten down and picked him up as you did." She shuddered suddenly. "It's one thing to joke about it. But that was truly the worst moment of my life. I think I'll have nightmares from here on out." Her eyes filled with sudden tears.

He put an arm around her shoulder and gave her a shake. "Hold on, Jenny. Don't go to pieces on me now. I'd really prefer that you keep on needling me. Remember what you were just saying. Tears aren't your style." He brushed a vagrant drop of water off her cheeks, then bent over to kiss the spot tenderly. It was no journey at all from there to her lips.

Later on, they could both attribute the next few minutes to nervous reaction. A spontaneous antidote to the harrowing experience that they'd been through. But for whatever reason, they found themselves kissing—passionately, ardently, frantically, desperately, and lengthily.

Only the sound of footsteps approaching up the stairs brought them to their senses. Jenny untangled herself, reluctantly, and rose unsteadily to her feet. Dalton tossed her bonnet, which had somehow become dislodged in the melee, up to her. She was smoothing the skirt of her pelisse, and he was pulling on his Hessians, when the approaching matron reached their floor.

The stout woman, puffing with the exertion of the climb, paused at the head of the stairs to catch her breath. Her mouth pursed in disapproval as she looked from one sheepish face to the other red one. Her sniff was eloquent as she continued her journey on down the corridor.

Jenny hoped she would soon learn to curb this deplorable tendency for giggling she was developing. At the moment it was well beyond control. "H-how's your manhood now?" she managed to utter between spasms.

"About two-thirds restored, I'd say." He grinned back as he offered her his arm.

" 'Two-thirds'? Is that all? Oh, I'd certainly give you higher marks than that."

They both struggled for composure as they proceeded arm in arm down the stairs and out into the street.

Chapter Twenty

PERHAPS IT WAS a guilty conscience that caused Jenny to dread an interview with her aunt. Lady Fremantle was indisposed. She hadn't left her bed-chamber the entire day. Jenny came into her presence with unaccustomed meekness and took a seat beside her bed.

There was no doubt that Lady Fremantle was displeased. The very fact that she'd demanded an interview before her abigail had done everything in her power to restore at least a reminder of her former beauty spoke to that. She sat propped up in bed, still in her nightgown and nightcap, sipping her tea while a plate of almond cakes remained untouched. The eye she fastened upon her eldest niece was baleful. Jenny braced herself.

"I'm most displeased with Sylvia."

"I beg your pardon?" Jenny's eyes widened in astonishment. That was the last thing she would have expected her aunt to say.

"You heard me, Jenny. I've no desire to keep repeating myself."

"Yes, ma'am. It's just that you amaze me. What could she possibly have done?"

"It's what she *hasn't* done that's the problem. Do

you realize that neither Lord Dalton nor Mr. Chalgrove has made an appearance here in a week?"

"I—err—really hadn't noticed." That was half true at any rate. Jenny was well aware that Dalton had not called at Fremantle House since he'd plucked little Earnest from off the ledge.

"Well, you should have done." Lady Fremantle's cup met its saucer with a peevish click. "Here they were, the two most eligible bachelors in all of London, dancing daily attendance upon Sylvia. All of my friends were remarking on it. Having *either* dangling after her would have been a triumph. But *both*!" For a moment her ladyship allowed herself to look triumphant before her face refell. "But now it has all come to nothing."

"Perhaps there's an explanation," Jenny offered. "They could be otherwise engaged. Or out of town."

"Both at the same time?" her ladyship snapped.

"Well, it could happen."

"The point is, if there is a reasonable explanation, Sylvia knows nothing of it. At least she *says* she knows no reason for it. Really, that girl is most exasperating. To have been blessed with all that beauty and not know how to use it! Why, any one of my sisters or myself would have had those gentlemen down on their knees in a fortnight. Really, I could shake her!"

"Well, perhaps they simply wouldn't suit," Jenny offered diffidently.

"Not suit!" Lady Fremantle's tone implied that her niece was bird-witted. "Each of those gentlemen is worth upward of twenty thousand pounds per annum. Of course they'd suit!"

"Yes, I do see what you mean," Jenny murmured. What she really didn't see was what her aunt expected her to do about it. She wasn't left long to wonder.

"I want you to have a talk with Sylvia. Find out exactly what's going on. Why, I shouldn't wonder if one—or both—of the gentlemen haven't already offered for her and the silly peagoose has turned them down. Really"—Lady Fremantle straightened her nightcap with a jerk—"I don't know what's wrong with you young women of today. It's nothing like my time, I can tell you."

"No, ma'am. I'm sure it isn't."

"And another thing." Her ladyship looked martyred. "As though I weren't distressed enough, now Fremantle is insisting that I arrange a musical evening and have Claire sing."

"Why, I think that's a famous notion."

"You do? Well, I'm not at all convinced. I don't know that it's a good idea to seem to be pushing Claire forward. Now I grant you that her appearance has improved—and I give myself full credit for doing what her mother should have done before foisting the girl off on me—but she's still far too plump to be considered a Beauty."

"But surely the point is, Aunt, that Claire sings like an angel."

"The point is to find a suitable husband for her. And, frankly, I'm not at all certain that she has the poise to carry off a performance. She's no good at all in company. Just sits there like a lump." Her ladyship shook her head. "No, I think it's a terrible notion and will no doubt end in disaster. But Fremantle insists. I vow I've never known him to be so stubborn over a thing. I wish you to speak to him as well."

Jenny was thinking furiously. "Do you know,

Aunt, a musical evening might be a very good notion at that. You could include Mr. Chalgrove and Lord Dalton in your invitations and give Sylvia a chance to mend her fences as it were. That is, if such a course of action is really necessary. And since the evening is in Claire's honor, they need not think that you are throwing Sylvia at their heads."

"Hmm." Lady Fremantle took a bite of almond cake and chewed it thoughtfully. "You may have a point," she observed thickly. "Just let me think on it a bit. In the meantime, you have a word with Sylvia."

But Sylvia was not to be found. She had slipped out of the house and was, at the moment, driving in the park with Captain St. Laurent.

She had been reluctant to do so. "Surely you aren't ashamed to be seen with me?" His handsome face looked hurt, and she'd hastened to deny it. "It just doesn't seem a good idea for us to be seen together. It might lead to questions."

"Who cares? We're old family friends, are we not? And I don't mind admitting that I'd like to meet your influential friends. There's my career to be considered. You do see that, don't you?"

She nodded. And tried not to look self-conscious as they drove through the park in his hired rig. The equipage was certainly not what she'd grown accustomed to. She tried not to make comparisons with Dalton and Chalgrove, for she knew it had set him back more than he could afford. She therefore did her best to make it appear that she was enjoying herself. But if the truth were known, she was hard put not to flinch every time they approached another carriage.

They did earn several curious looks and nods from mere acquaintances. But Sylvia had just begun to think that they might actually leave Hyde Park without seeing anyone whom she knew well when she saw a familiar-looking curricle approaching. Her heart sank a bit as she spied the Honorable Reggie York-Jones holding the reins. It plummeted even farther when she discovered that it was Lady Warrington with him.

Reggie had been much in that lady's company of late. He was under no illusion as to why. He was on intimate terms with Lord Dalton, and it was common knowledge that Lady Warrington was wearing the willow for that gentleman. Indeed, she did seem to spend most of their time together pumping him about Dalton's activities. He frankly found it all a bore. But he was most anxious to become a man about town, and, being seen in Lady Warrington's company boosted that ambition, so he put up with it.

"Oh, look," she cooed in his ear as their curricle approached the rented rig. "I can hardly believe my eyes. That's Lady Sylvia Kinnard on that shabby gig. But who is the Adonis with her? Oh, do stop, Reggie, dear."

Sylvia tried not to sound uneasy as she made the introductions. But the truth was, Lady Warrington's overdone cordiality filled her with apprehension. She was well aware that the lady had no cause to like her. She found her open flirtation with the captain most suspect. "A family friend and a newcomer to the metropolis. Shame on you, Lady Sylvia, for keeping this military hero hidden. I shall see to it, sir, that you no longer remain her ladyship's exclusive property. After all, she has enough

164

gentlemen at her feet." Here she was unable to keep a note of spite from creeping in. "I shall personally see to it that you begin to circulate, Captain St. Laurent."

"What a charming lady," the captain exclaimed after the gig and curricle had gone their separate ways. "And such a Beauty."

When Sylvia didn't answer, he gave her a searching look. "Oh, come now. Surely you're not jealous."

"Of course not. I just wonder what she's up to, that's all."

"That doesn't sound at all like you, Sylvia. Surely you can't begrudge me the chance to make a bit of a splash on my own? After all, as the lady said, you've all of London at your feet."

"N-no. Of course I don't. Just be on your guard, that's all."

"Oh, don't worry, m'dear." He flipped his reins to urge his sluggish cattle out into the traffic of Park Lane. "I'm the soul of discretion. You surely must know that by now."

For his part, Reginald York-Jones couldn't see why Lady Warrington was so elated over meeting Captain St. Laurent. If the truth were known, the fellow had struck him as something of a mushroom. Not quite the thing, somehow. Didn't seem up to Lady Sylvia's standards. But then, of course, he was a handsome fellow. And females valued that sort of thing. Still, Reggie thought, it wouldn't hurt to make some inquiries. He knew two or three chaps in the captain's regiment. Made sense to find out a bit about the fellow.

But after he'd taken Lady Warrington home and

returned to his rooms in Bird Street, a new development pushed Captain St. Laurent completely from his nonretentive mind. Among the letters and invitations awaiting him on a silver tray was a missive with the Earl of Rexford's seal pressed into the wax. Reggie tore it open and perused it three times before he actually comprehended what he'd read. "Now that's deuced odd," he muttered to himself.

Chapter Twenty-one

TWO BRIGHT SPOTS glowed in Claire's cheeks. Except for this telltale evidence, she seemed the soul of calm. Both cousins had come to her room to supervise her toilette, a bit of attention that the abigail, putting the last touches on a Grecian coiffure, could have done without.

"We want you to wear these. For luck, you know." Jenny handed the abigail her single-strand pearl necklace and Sylvia's pearl eardrops. "Not that you need luck," she hurried on to explain.

"No," Sylvia added, "we simply like the notion of being a part of your triumph."

Claire managed a wan smile. "You two are being marvelous. And I do appreciate your support, believe me. But I don't think you need worry. I passed being frightened ages ago. I've proceeded on to numb. Now hadn't you best be going? Guests should arrive at any moment and Aunt will have your heads if you aren't there to help receive. There's one thing about being the featured attraction of the evening. I am spared that."

Lord Fremantle, also intent upon Claire's wellbeing, stopped Jenny for a private word as she and Sylvia left the room.

"I have a favor to ask, Cousin Jenny."

"Certainly. Anything." She suspected that underneath his usual calm exterior he was more nervous than Claire. She liked him for it immensely.

"I've asked Lord Hazlett here tonight—" he began.

"You've *what*?"

"Sssssh" Her voice had risen inadvertently. "I thought it important to Claire that she be on good terms with her father. But I don't wish her to have added pressure during her performance. So could you see to his lordship, Cousin Jenny, and keep him out of sight until Claire has performed?"

Just how she was to accomplish such a feat was beyond imagining. Hide him behind a potted palm? Give him a loo mask? She kept all such reservations to herself, however, and managed an encouraging smile. "Why, yes, of course, Cousin James. I'll be happy to do so."

"Where is Fremantle?" Her aunt was fuming when Jenny joined her and Sylvia by the drawing-room door. "People will begin arriving at any moment."

"He's on his way. He just wanted to wish Claire luck."

"Having palpitations is she? Well, never mind. I've seen to it that we also have professional musicians on hand."

The sound of the doorbell cut off the retort Jenny longed to make.

Reginald York-Jones was among the first arrivals. Jenny thought he looked rather tired and drawn. And for some reason he did not meet her eyes. "Are you feeling quite the thing?" she inquired solicitously.

"Oh, yes. Never better, in fact," he told the jet lozenges that trimmed her bustline.

She was kept from wondering about his odd behavior by the sight of Lord Dalton, who was bending over her aunt's hand. This would be their first encounter since the rescue of Earnest with its curious aftermath. She hoped she'd not do anything foolish like blushing when he approached. Her voice, at any rate, didn't quiver when her turn came and she said for his ears alone, "I need to have a private word with you."

"Yes, I expect you do," he said dryly.

"Oh, don't be an ass. It's not what you're no doubt thinking."

"I don't see how you could possibly know what I'm thinking." He then was forced to move along and greet Sylvia.

Even though she managed to smile at him, there seemed some restraint on that young lady's part. Lord Dalton, with difficulty, suppressed a sigh. He was in for a long evening, it seemed.

Lord Hazlett arrived late. On purpose. Lady Fremantle had already taken her place upon the temporary platform erected at one end of the drawing room and was preparing the fifty or so assembled guests for the musical treat ahead. Jenny, still lurking in the hall, turned to greet him. "Uncle, I'd almost given you up."

"I thought it might be more . . . politic to just slip in unobserved."

They didn't quite succeed in this, however. Lady Fremantle saw them taking their places in the very back of the rows of rout chairs and was momentarily thrown into confusion. She managed to recover her aplomb, however, and, before any of the guests were moved to wonder at her odd reaction, went on praising the harpist and baritone that they were privileged to hear. "My niece will also sing for you," she added, apparently as an afterthought.

The harpist began. And as far as Jenny was concerned, played interminably. Then came the baritone. Jenny squirmed impatiently throughout his solo. She even grew oblivious to her uncle's presence in her anxiety for Claire. Lord Dalton was looking at her from the row just in front of hers and across the center aisle. Her nervousness must be showing, she concluded as she tried to compose her features. Dalton looked away.

When the polite applause for the baritone had faded, Lady Fremantle rose from her position in the front row of chairs and turned toward her guests. "My niece, Lady Claire, will now sing for you," she announced, then shot a darkling look toward the young lady's father. Without realizing she was doing so, Jenny clutched her uncle's hand.

It was obvious to those who knew her best, that Claire was nervous. The red spots in her cheeks glowed brightly and the gloved hands, clasped together at her waist, trembled ever so slightly. But even as Jenny's grip on her uncle's hand became viselike, she could not help noticing with pride how very nice Claire looked. The blue net gown she wore, chosen of course by Sylvia, was most becoming. And no one could now consider her more than "pleasingly plump."

Lord Fremantle had set aside his aversion to public performance and agreed to accompany Lady Claire. Indeed, that had been the only way to persuade her to perform. Now he played an introduction and smiled encouragingly. As the smile lit his usually grave face, Claire visibly relaxed. And so did Jenny.

Fremantle had chosen her music carefully. Claire began with a ballad, lovely, but undemanding. The applause was enthusiastic. She looked abashed at first and then seemed pleased. The next selection, an aria, was chosen with an eye to showing off her range and artistry. She sang as though inspired; every note was clear and true.

The applause was thunderous. The dangling prisms in the huge crystal chandelier above them danced in rhythm with it. The ovation would have been tumultuous under any circumstance, Jenny was certain, but it lost nothing from the fact that Lord Hazlett so completely forgot himself as to leap to his feet and lead it. His "Bravo" resounded above all the rest.

Claire could not fail to see him. She appeared thunderstruck at first, but then she smiled shyly in her father's direction. Jenny felt her eyes begin to moisten. You peagoose, she chided herself, and went on clapping.

"Your cousin was a triumph." At the end of the concert, when the other guests were collected around Claire, Lord Dalton spoke at Jenny's elbow.

"Yes, I see she even kept you awake. Listen, I have to talk to you."

"So you said. Here I am."

"Not here. Privately. Come on. Let's slip away while no one's noticing us."

She closed the library door behind them, then turned to face him. The often rehearsed words came out in a rush. "I think we ought to clear up something right away. There's no need for you to avoid

171

Sylvia on my account. If you think I've said one word about that—trivial incident—after you'd saved Earnest, you much mistake the matter. I wouldn't dream of such a thing. Nor would I overblow it. We were neither one ourselves. It is best forgotten. And, I assure you, for my part, it would have been already . . . but for the fact that you've become—well, conspicuous by your absence. My aunt has commented on it. And while Sylvia would never speak of her feelings, I'm sure she must be wondering why you are avoiding her."

There was a long, intense moment of silence. Lord Dalton, lounging back against the bookcase with an elbow resting on a shelf, stared at her. Only her height seemed to prevent his looking down his nose.

" *'Trivial incident'?*" he asked.

"I beg your pardon?"

"You said you hadn't told your cousin about the *trivial incident*. Is that truly what you considered it?"

"Well, naturally."

"You mean that it's *natural* for you to sit passionately kissing on a dirty landing in a business establishment while interested onlookers mill back and forth? You do shock me, Miss Blythe."

Her cheeks flamed. "That was a shabby thing to say. And no *'onlookers'* milled back and forth. There was only one odious woman."

"I stand corrected. Just one spectator *would* trivialize the incident, of course."

"I do wish you'd quit harping on that phrase!" she snapped. "You seem to completely fail to take my point. It's Sylvia who's at issue here."

"Obviously." His face was enigmatic.

"I do not wish you to feel any constraint there on

my account. I am not laying any claims upon your affection because of an unguarded moment, Lord Dalton. And I hold myself more to blame than you for the incident."

"*Trivial* incident," he corrected.

"For what happened. Do I make myself clear?"

"Abundantly."

"Well, then," she said crossly, "I don't know why you are being so odiously starchy. I thought you'd be relieved. To speak plainly, I haven't seen you behave like this since you lectured me at Almack's. I did think, m'lord, that we'd progressed beyond that."

"Oh, yes. I'd say we'd progressed *a great deal* beyond that."

"Quit echoing everything I say. I do beg pardon if I've offended you—though I don't see how I could have done. I have never before felt constrained to stand on points with you, and certainly didn't see a need to begin now."

"No need whatsoever."

"Then will you speak to Sylvia?"

" 'Speak to Sylvia?' " His eyebrows shot up. "Are you suggesting that I go down on one knee, Miss Blythe?"

"I'm suggesting nothing beyond this one simple thing—that I've tried, with little success I fear, to make you understand." She deliberately dragged out her words. "There-is-no-need-to-shun-Sylvia-on-my-account. Now is that clear?"

"Perfectly, Miss Blythe. Don't you think we should join the others before someone wrongly concludes that another *trivial incident* is taking place?"

He moved to open the library door ... and gave

a mocking bow as she swept by him with an angry glare.

Lord Dalton was in no mood to stay for the lavish supper that would conclude the evening's entertainment. He was striding toward Mount Street in something approaching high dudgeon when he heard footsteps hurrying behind him. "Dalton! Wait up!" Reggie York-Jones called.

Dalton was not overjoyed. His tone was less than cordial. "Never knew you to leave a party before the refreshments, Reggie."

"Well, I had to talk to you, didn't I? And I saw you streak out of there as if your tailcoat was on fire."

"Can't it wait?" Dalton sighed.

"Well, no, it can't, I'm afraid." Reggie struggled with himself and then lost. "Look here, old fellow. I'm supposed to pump you subtly and find out some things for your father. But I'm no good at that sort of havey-cavey business. Seems best to just come right out and ask you. But, I say, do we have to go on standing here?"

After they had settled in front of a crackling fire in his lordship's parlor with a bottle of claret between them, Dalton, who was sprawled in a wing chair opposite Reggie's with his feet stretched to the blaze, inquired, "Now do I have this straight? My father wrote asking you to worm some information out of me?"

"No, no. That is to say, he didn't write. He asked me."

Dalton sat up straight. "Papa's here in London? And he didn't want me to know?" He looked stricken. "Oh, God, he must be worse. I collect he came up to consult with his doctor."

"Well, no. At least he may have done that, too. But he mainly came up to see Harriet Wilson."

"He did *what*? I'll not believe it."

Harriet Wilson was the most fashionable courtesan in London. Her clientele was made up exclusively of the pink of the ton. The Dukes of Wellington and Argyll, among others, were her regular visitors.

That Reggie was well aware of this was reflected in the smug expression that now suffused his boyish face. "You'd best believe it. Harry—by the by, that's what she asked me to call her, don't you know—Harry doesn't see just anybody. But your father's a particular favorite of hers, she said.

"Now wait just a minute, York-Jones. You aren't going to tell me that Papa—in his condition—actually went to bed with Harriet Wilson."

"Why, no, I'm not."

"I should think not."

"No, for he asked her as a particular favor to take me in his place." The young man turned suddenly pink. "Initiate me, as it were."

"I see," Dalton said dryly.

"That was deuced nice of him, you must admit, for Harriet would never as a usual thing—err—entertain the likes of me. She prefers her gentlemen well established, she said. But I don't know what you mean about your papa's condition. He—ah—went with Harriet's sister Fanny, you see. And afterward, when we all had a late supper together, she went on and on about how exhausted she was. And how your papa put all the young men to shame. Harriet—*Harry*, I mean to say, laughed and said that she took all the credit. That she'd been governess to him for years and had certainly taught him a trick or two."

Lord Dalton was suddenly looking dangerous. "She said that, did she? Oh, you must have been a jolly little group."

"Oh, we were. The best," York-Jones replied enthusiastically. "I'd always been in awe of your father, Dalton. Don't mind saying that even though he is my godfather, he always made me quiver in me boots. But he really is a right 'un, I must say."

"A regular life of the party, I take it."

"Oh, yes. Last thing I would have expected, like I said. Treated me just like a son."

"Not exactly." The tone was even dryer.

"You don't mean to say! You surely ain't implying that Lord Rexford never took *you* to Harry's."

"Not even once."

"Well, I'm dashed."

There was a pregnant silence. Both men seemed rocked by recent revelations.

"Well," Reggie was finally moved to say, "I collect that makes it even more important for me to find out what his lordship wants to know."

"Which is?"

"How your suit is prospering. Those are his words, not mine. Seems he has his heart set on your marrying Caro Percival's daughter. I told him that as far as I knew you were going about the business in first-rate fashion. But he wants me to find out whether you've gone down on one knee yet. And if you've not, just when you plan to. What shall I tell him?" He paused expectantly.

It was on the tip of Dalton's tongue to tell his esteemed parent to go to the devil, but he bit back the words and rose to his feet instead. "Go home, Reggie."

"Oh, but you have to give me an answer, Dalton." York-Jones was obviously distressed. "I mean to say, I can't let his lordship down. Not after Harriet Wilson. Surely you must see that."

"Hmm. Well, yes, I suppose you are rather on the spot." He stood a moment in frowning thought. "Very well, then. You can tell my father that I mean to make an offer of marriage at the first opportunity."

"Oh, I say!" The young man leaped to his feet and began pumping Dalton's arm up and down. "That really is famous, by Jove. And to think I get to be the first to wish you happy!"

"A bit premature, but thank you all the same. Now go home, Reggie. I have a call to make first thing in the morning."

Chapter Twenty-two

"MY GOD!"

Lord Dalton had at last located Mr. Chalgrove. He had gone first to White's, then to Boodle's, and on to Brook's. The last place he'd expected to find him was in his own rooms. Nor in his wildest dreams would he have expected to find this pattern card for aspiring Corinthians looking so disheveled. At nine o'clock in the evening he was still wearing his nightclothes and dressing gown. He was unshaven and, so Dalton suspected, unwashed. He was seated, gazing morosely at the fire with a wine decanter at his elbow. Dalton noticed—with a measure of relief—that it appeared to be untouched. "I say, are you sickening for something?" he asked.

"No, of course not." The dandy didn't bother to turn his head and look at his visitor. "I just happen to prefer my own company at the moment. Go away."

"I'll do nothing of the sort. I've come to take you to Almack's. Hurry up and get ready. We don't have all that much time."

At least he got his host's full attention. The gaze was stony. "Whatever put such a maggot in your head, Dalton? I've no intention of going to Al-

178

mack's. Tonight or any night. Ever. Going to Almack's was the biggest mistake of my life."

"Hmm." Lord Dalton, towering above the seated man, studied him carefully. "Well, I see that I was right. You are well and truly smitten. Get dressed, Roderick. You are going. For I badly need you to get me off the hook."

"Oh, and just what hook is that? Not that I intend to move a muscle, mind you."

"The matrimonial hook. As you, and everyone else in town, are aware of, I've been pursuing Lady Sylvia for weeks now with an eye toward marriage. But now I've discovered that there's no need for such drastic action. It was all my dear father's idea, you see. His dying request. Or so he put it. But this morning I visited his London quack and found out that the old fraud is healthy as a horse and will probably outlive me. So I don't intend to become a Tenant for Life just to please his lying lordship. But the problem is, it wouldn't be the thing just to drop Lady Sylvia. So that's where you come in, my dear fellow."

Mr. Chalgrove's attention had been rapt. But his expression was not encouraging. "It's a bit difficult for me to imagine why," he drawled.

"That should be obvious. There's no question that you have a *tendre* for the girl. In fact, you look ready to die of it. You know, if my own case weren't so desperate, I'd actually be enjoying this. But the thing is, Chalgrove, I need you to get in there ahead of me and offer for Lady Sylvia. That would fix everything right and tight. No one could think the worse of the girl for accepting you. You're almost as good a catch as I am."

" 'Almost'?" Chalgrove's eyebrows rose. Despite

his unkempt appearance he managed to look himself again.

"Almost," Lord Dalton repeated firmly. "Your fortune may be as good. Or better? And I will admit that females seem to find you handsome, though God knows why. But you mustn't forget my title. In the female mind that always tips the scale. Aside from all that," he said musingly, "I've had the impression that this little gudgeon"—he ignored Chalgrove's dangerous frown—"actually prefers you over me. Which is another reason for my not going down on one knee. I'd hate like the very devil to wind up leg-shackled to someone with so little taste."

"Never fear. You won't be."

"Ah, that's the spirit. Come now. Get into your evening clothes and it's on to Almack's."

"Skip your cursed exhortation to the troops, Dalton. You miss my point entirely. Lady Sylvia's not going to marry you *or* me. She's in love with someone else."

That was a leveler. Uninvited, Dalton pulled up a chair and collapsed in it. "I'll not believe it."

"Well, you'd better. She's been meeting the fellow on the sly. Some military cove she knew on the continent.

"So you were never really on the hook, old man. She's played us both for fools. You can go down on one knee till it gets rheumatism and she still won't have you. So go on"—he waved dismissively—"get out of here, make your offer, and leave me in peace."

Dalton was thinking furiously. "Don't expect me to be that rash. She wouldn't be the first female to let love go chase itself when a title and fortune got dangled before her. Take my word for it, 'all for love's' more honored in the breach than the observance."

"Not Lady Sylvia!"

"No need to look so murderous. Your loyalty does you credit. But will you answer me two things?" Without waiting for Chalgrove's permission, he proceeded. "First, how did you learn of her attachment to this fellow?"

"From Emily Warrington."

Dalton's lip curled. "And you believed that malicious doxy? I say, Chalgrove, you are losing your touch. Now for the second question. Are you in love with Lady Sylvia?"

"That's none of your damn business."

"So I was right. You are then." Dalton seemed satisfied with his probing. "Come on. Get dressed. You've wasted enough of my time already."

"But you don't understand, Dalton." Chalgrove's customary haughty expression had been exchanged for abject misery. "She told me that she never wants to see me again."

"Did she, by Jove?" Dalton visibly brightened. "Well, that *is* good news. Sounds like she may actually be in love with you."

"Have you lost your senses?"

"Not at all. You see, the trouble with you women-hating coves is that you never gain any experience of the way the feminine mind works. Then, when you finally do get smitten, you're completely out of your depth."

He got up, walked to the mantle, and pulled the bell rope.

"Just what do you think you're doing?"

"Calling your man. We're going to Almack's even

if I have to hold you down while your valet dresses you."

The young ladies of Grosvenor Square were only slightly less reluctant to visit Almack's than Mr. Chalgrove. But Lady Fremantle met their demurs with a rush of indignation. "Not go? Of course you will go! Do you realize that the Season is nearly over and not one of you has had an offer? I vow I'll never be able to show my face in Society again. I'll be forced to take up residence in the country, and if there is one thing I cannot abide, it's the country. And what is more, my sisters are bound to blame me for the fact that the three of you have not found husbands. Though who could have made a greater push than I have, I'd like to know? And without one of them so much as lifting a finger! Why, just look at what I've done for you alone, Claire. You certainly are not the same hopeless case you were before I took you under my wing, now are you?"

"No, ma'am." Claire's face remained composed, but her eyes twinkled as they met her tall cousin's.

Except for claiming credit, for once my aunt is right, Jenny mused. Claire has changed. Almost beyond recognition. And not primarily in appearance, though she has slimmed down a great deal. The real change comes from within. She seems confident. And happy. The reunion with her father has done wonders for her.

She was snapped out of her reverie by her aunt's summation. "We will indeed go to Almack's tonight. And the three of you shall be at pains to make yourselves agreeable to any eligible gentlemen present or I shall be most displeased."

* * *

The contrast to their first visit to the Assembly Rooms was striking. The cousins were no longer a curiosity. Indeed, they had quite a few friends among the assembled ton. It was no longer necessary for the patronesses to steer eligible young men their way. None of them lacked for partners. Claire, particularly, was experiencing a change of fortune. Several gentlemen present revised their earlier impressions of her appearance and recalled the sizable fortune that came with this only child. And, noting the absence of those two formidable rivals, Lord Dalton and Mr. Chalgrove, other gentlemen, who had been too intimidated at other times, now vied for the chance to stand up with the trio's beauty, Lady Sylvia.

Jenny did not quite achieve the popularity of the other two. She had her admirers, but her height and her insightful wit put off the more faint of heart. York-Jones, however, was not among their number. One night with Harriet Wilson had made him feel equal to anything. During a rather long lull in the course of a country dance, he proposed.

No sooner were the fatal words out of his mouth than Jenny was swept away from him. "Well?" he asked when they were once more reunited.

"Well, what?"

"You know," he whispered frowning. "Will you?"

She sighed and looked down at him with tender exasperation. "I was sure that I'd misheard you. Nobody, Reggie, would actually make an offer during a country dance. And at Almack's of all places."

"Well, I didn't know when else I might see you privately."

"And you might not get up the nerve again?" she ventured.

His denial was spoiled slightly by his blush.

Once more, they were involved in the dance figure. "Whatever put such a maggot in your brain?" she asked when they came together.

"It's not a maggot. I've been thinking of it all along. And Lord Rexford himself said it was time I married."

"Lord Rexford? Dalton's father?"

The small man nodded.

"What does he have to say to anything?"

"He's my godfather, didn't you know?"

The dance came to an end. As he escorted his partner back to her chair, York-Jones whispered, "You don't have to give me an answer now. Just promise you'll think about it."

"Oh, there's no need for thought. I can give you my answer now. It's no. Despite the great Lord Rexford, you're far too young to think of marriage to anyone. And as for marrying me, the fact is, I do happen to love you. Like a brother. And what's more, I have the perfect young lady in mind for you, my little sister Elizabeth. She'll make her bow in three years time. And if I may be permitted to boast, I collect she may cast even our cousin Sylvia in the shade. And, no, she is not a Long Meg like me."

"Oh, I say," he protested.

"No, you don't say. But what you will do is wait for Elizabeth." Jenny could not believe just how much she sounded like her aunt.

Lord Dalton and Mr. Chalgrove created their usual sensation when they made their appearance. Mr. Chalgrove resisted all efforts to be paired with a dancing partner. "We came only for the refreshments," he told a patroness solemnly. "Who could resist the lure of weak lemonade and stale cake?"

Lord Dalton was, however, more conforming. He whisked Lady Sylvia out from under a prospective partner's nose and took the floor with her.

As he watched the handsome couple dance, Chalgrove concentrated upon keeping his face a blank. His success was only moderate, evidently. "I wouldn't give a penny for your thoughts," a brittle voice spoke at his elbow. "I can't begin to tell you how wearied I've become from watching all the men in this town make cakes of themselves over that Kinnard chit." He turned to find Lady Warrington there beside him.

"Jealousy doesn't become you, Emily," he drawled. "It's frightfully bad ton, you know."

"Oh, I'm not jealous in the least, I can assure you. It's just that I find all of this second-generation Percival lore tedious to the extreme. Tedious *and* ridiculous. Did you know that— But, no. I do have the most delicious *on-dit* to tell, but I promised Lady Jersey she should hear it first. Do come along, though, Chalgrove. This is a bit of gossip you won't want to miss." She took his arm.

The dancers left the floor. Lord Dalton escorted Lady Sylvia to a chair next to Claire and Jenny and, with the Honorable Reggie York-Jones and Lord Fremantle, went for refreshments. Lady Warrington, with Chalgrove still in tow, drew Lady Jersey and the entourage around her to one side. She took care to position her group within easy earshot of the cousins.

After the gentlemen had returned bearing tepid lemonade, the conversation lagged. Lady Sylvia, who rarely had much to say in any case, seemed all too conscious of Mr. Chalgrove's proximity. Lord Dalton was too engaged in assessing this reaction to contribute much in the way of small talk. Lord Fremantle appeared uncharacteristically blue-deviled. He had seldom strung three words together throughout the evening. Claire watched him anxiously. And the usually garrulous York-Jones was at a loss whether to be cast down or relieved over his rejected marriage offer. After a few failed attempts to get a conversation going, Jenny had given up, and, without much interest, was watching the dancing.

Then the name "Percival," spoken in a mocking tone, caught all their attention. It was impossible thereafter to miss a word of what Lady Warrington was telling the group collected around her, lured by the prospect of hearing the "juiciest scandal to come this way for years."

"The entire business is enough to send me into the whoops just to think on it," she was saying. "The *fabulous* Percivals. Almack's own version of the Cinderella story. Here came these penniless beauties out of the Irish—or was it the Welsh?—cinders. And each captivated a handsome prince. Am I not right? Isn't that how the story goes? And were they not, then, to live happily ever after in the best fairy-tale tradition? Well, my dears"—she looked around the group in a conspiratorial manner and lowered her voice; it seemed to lose none of its histrionic carrying power, however—"so much for happy endings. I have it on good authority that every one of those marriages ended in disaster.

"Well, to be fair," she qualified, with a straight face, though her eyes sparked mischief, "I should except our own dear Lady Fremantle. After all, her

186

spouse was considerate enough to die in two years time and leave her a very wealthy woman. Her case, I'll grant, carried on the fairy-tale tradition."

The group around her tittered appreciatively. Lord Fremantle's head turned angrily, but Claire had laid a restraining hand upon his sleeve.

"And of course everyone in town knows all about Lord Hazlett's mistress and little bastards. So much for *that* Percival's happy marriage. And as for the one in the north—the Long Meg's mother—I understand that the poor dear breeds more often than the gamekeeper's rabbits. But, then, you must know all that. It's the latest scandal I wished to tell you."

Jenny heard Sylvia's sudden intake of breath and looked her way. She had gone white as chalk. Jenny just stopped herself from reaching out to take her hand. Such an impulsive action would only call attention to her cousin's distress.

"A friend of mine just let the cat out of the bag," Lady Warrington was saying, with obvious relish. "Vienna has been abuzz with the scandal. It has quite eclipsed all political matters. Everything pales beside the news that the fourth Percival—our own dear Lady Sylvia's mother—has thrown her cap over the windmill, deserted her husband—whom she's been cuckolding for years, so they say—and has run off to Paris with a cavalry officer who's at least ten years younger than she . . . and has left a wife and two little ones behind. Now I ask you, is that not the last ironic touch? Indeed if that does not write finis to all of this absurd Percival nonsense, then, my dears, I for one cannot imagine what it will take."

Lady Warrington paused to enjoy the sensation she'd created. Her audience was looking appropri-

187

ately shocked and began stealing glances at the Percival daughters, trying to ascertain whether they'd overheard. Mr. Chalgrove broke the silence.

"Emily, dear." His tone was solicitous. "You must allow me to summon your carriage."

"Whatever for? I've certainly no intention of leaving yet."

"But my dear lady, you surely cannot contemplate staying here a moment longer with the front of that lovely gown of yours soaked with lemonade."

Lady Warrington glanced hastily down at her modish Urling's lace creation. "Have you taken leave of your senses, Chalgrove? There's no lemonade on my gown."

He raised his quizzing glass and peered closer. "By Jove, you're right." His voice was redolent of surprise. "Well, now, that's easily remedied." And he slowly, deliberately, to the accompaniment of an entire chorus of shocked gasps, emptied the contents of the glass he held down her ladyship's décolletage.

Chalgrove took no notice of the ringing slap across his cheek. Instead, he turned toward Jenny, bowing gracefully, and raised his empty glass in a salute. "My gratitude, Miss Blythe," he called out to her. "Now, thanks to you, I've at last discovered a proper use for this insipid, undrinkable concoction."

Chapter Twenty-three

LADY CLAIRE FOLLOWED the strains of music to their source. The melody was somber, as befitted the mood of Fremantle House.

Lord Fremantle glanced up from the keyboard as she entered the room. His smile was rather forced. "I hope my music didn't disturb you. I've been trying to play softly. Is anyone else up?"

"Your playing could never disturb me." She came to stand by the pianoforte. "And I'm the only one up. Or at least the only one to have left her room. Please don't let me interrupt you. We do need music."

"How is Cousin Sylvia taking all of this?" He continued to play softly.

"It's difficult to say. Last night she told us that she had known about her mother's affair before she came here. She had wished to stay home with her father, but he'd insisted that she make her come-out. He wanted her to behave as if nothing had happened. It was his opinion that the scandal wouldn't reach London. At least not until the Season was over. But Sylvia has been braced since her arrival for the ax to fall at any moment. Especially when Captain St. Laurent arrived in London. She was terrified that he'd let the cat out of the bag. He had given her his word that he wouldn't mention it, but that odious Lady Warrington wormed it out of him."

"She would." Lord Fremantle forgot himself and struck a dissonant chord.

"Sylvia has been convinced that the scandal would make her ineligible for a brilliant marriage. That's why she never encouraged any of her suitors. She felt it would be dishonest to do so."

"That's absurd, of course. No right-thinking man would give a fig."

She smiled at him. "Yes, but one gets the impression that right-thinking men are rather scarce in London."

"Oh, come now. Aren't you a bit hard on us males?"

"Never on you, Cousin James. But tell me. I was thinking of having a talk with Sylvia later in the day. Do you think I should? She is so very reserved, she might feel it an intrusion. Then, too, Jenny is much better than I at this sort of thing. We both look up to her."

"And rightly so. But not in this instance," his lordship said firmly. "You are the very one to talk to her, Claire."

"I'll do it then if you think I should," she said resolutely.

He played on softly for a few moments, then asked casually, "I collect that you will all be leaving soon, then?"

"Yes. I do think last night put a period to our Season." She smiled wryly. "Poor Aunt Fremantle is utterly prostrated by the whole business, you know." She laughed suddenly. "She even went so far as to blame Jenny for the fact that Mr. Chalgrove has been barred from Almack's for life. Aunt says that he never would have thought of such a shocking thing without her example."

Fremantle laughed, too. "Oh, I don't know. He's an inventive man, I collect. And the choices are limited. One cannot, after all, challenge a female to a duel or give her a leveler. Though I must say that for the one and only time in my life I quite longed to."

"You? Well, that just goes to show the lengths you've been driven to by our invasion of your orderly life." She couldn't quite bring herself to look at him. "I collect you'll be relieved to see the last of your troublesome cousins."

"Quite the contrary," he said huskily. "I shall hate it above all things. I don't think I've ever spent such a happy time. In fact, I know I haven't.

"And what about you, Claire? Will you be glad to leave? I know you didn't wish to come, but has it been so bad for you?"

"Oh, no. In fact, it's been the most marvelous thing that has ever happened to me."

"Yes, there's no denying your success." His smile was forced. "I watched you last night, you know, with all the young gentlemen flocking around you. I can't believe that any Percival sister was ever more sought after."

"You exaggerate. But no matter. For the point is, that although I never in my wildest dreams expected such a thing to happen, I've fallen in love."

Lord Fremantle looked as if he'd just received a mortal blow. But he managed to keep his voice steady. "Well, then, I, of course, am happy for you. And who is the fortunate fellow? If you don't mind saying, that is."

"Why, you, of course."

"I b-beg your pardon?"

"Oh, I know it's a shocking thing to say, James. And I realize your regard for me is—cousinly. But I did want you to know. For I feel that even though you are such a tower of strength to everyone around you"—tears filled her eyes—"and no one could have been kinder to me than you have been, I do believe that in many ways you undervalue yourself . . . prodigiously. So in the teeth of maidenly modesty, I had to tell you that you are—and always shall be— my beau ideal.

"Now I know I've embarrassed you terribly. And you must not concern yourself that I shall ever regret such plain speaking. For thanks to you, I am not that same quaking, self-loathing creature that I was. I shall be all right. Truly."

"Are you certain that you aren't confusing gratitude—a *misplaced* gratitude at that—for love? You were always beautiful, Claire. You just didn't realize it."

"I do know you truly thought so. Which made you a candidate for a straightjacket of course. But it meant everything to me that you saw more than— or should I say *less* than"—she grimaced—"just the surface."

"I was very little ahead of the others in realizing what a superior person you are. Your kindness. Your talent. Your sense of humor. All these things eclipse even your physical beauty. You do realize that you can have any man in London, don't you?"

"Not unless *you* offer for me."

"Are you serious?" He looked unbelieving. "You'd actually settle for a dull dog like me?"

"No, I'd not '*settle*.' I wish to marry you above all

192

things. And if you don't feel the same—well, I won't kill myself or eat myself obese or enter a convent or anything else of the kind. But I won't ever marry. You may be sure of that. For no one—*no* one—can ever hope to measure up to you, James."

"I'd—I'd—no idea. Oh, Claire, my dearest Claire. I don't doubt that I've been in love with you from the moment we first met. But it never occurred to me that you felt the same."

"Oh, James, you peagoose. I said that you were hopeless. Now it's shocking enough that I've actually proposed to you. Oh, please, my darling, don't make me kiss you as well. I'd never be able to face myself in the glass again after such rackety behavior."

Lord Fremantle needed no more prodding. He jumped up from the pianoforte and folded her in his arms.

Lady Fremantle's majordomo had been fully engaged in turning away morning callers. "Her Ladyship and the young ladies are not at home," he announced time after time to the would-be gossipmongers who were dying to assess the full damage caused by the scandal that had broken at Almack's. London had seen nothing like it for years. No one would soon forget this Season. But the curious had to content themselves with the satisfaction of being able to report at their next port of call that toplofty Lydia Fremantle was too humiliated to show her face.

Mr. Chalgrove was not so easily put off, however. He pushed past Jackson impatiently, and, over the butler's protests, handed him his greatcoat, hat, and cane. He was running up the stairs as Jenny was coming down them. "Where is she?" he demanded.

Her eyebrows rose, but for once she bridled her tongue. "The first door on the right," she told him.

"Come in." A listless voice answered his preemptive knock. Lady Sylvia was seated on the window seat, her legs tucked up underneath her skirts, looking out at the leaden skies that so aptly reflected her frame of mind. She glanced with disinterest over her shoulder. Then her eyes widened with shock.

Chalgrove closed the door softly behind him and leaned against it. "Will you marry me?" he asked.

She pretended not to have heard the question. "I'm truly sorry, Mr. Chalgrove, that you were barred from Almack's on my account. I wish there was some way I could make amends."

He strode across the room to sit beside her and clasp both her hands in his. "There is. Marry me. Then we can both not go to Almack's together."

She managed a smile. "I must confess I'm glad that I never have to see that odious place again. But please don't feel sorry for me, Mr. Chalgrove—" Her voice broke. "I don't think I could bear that."

"I don't feel sorry for you," he said impatiently. "Oh, well, dammit . . . I do feel bad that you're obviously miserable, but that's because I love you and has nothing to do with those tabbies who are chewing us up right now while they drink their scandal broth. Those people are beneath contempt, my darling. And you should not mind them in the least."

Her steady gaze seemed to pierce right through him. "That's an odd speech for you to make, sir. It was my impression that you, above all people, savored a good scandal. And that you would never be able to tolerate becoming an object of sport yourself. You've been used to being the conveyer of gossip, never its subject."

He reddened. "Sylvia, I've done a lot of shabby things in my lifetime. But none, believe me, that I regret so deeply as hurting your cousin. I know you have every right to hold me in contempt. I know that I'm not nearly good enough for you. But I will try and change. Oh, I realize that people who make that sort of statement rarely do, but, honestly, my darling, I have the highest hopes in my case. You see, I'd always thought it quite impossible for me to fall in love. And—well, now that I've managed that without so much as trying, I can't help but feel that all things are possible. Will you marry me?"

She gazed at him with wonder. "You really do love me?"

"With all my heart. Tell me. Am I going about this proposal business all wrong? I've never given it the slightest thought you see. I'm quite a high-stickler in other things. But in affairs of the heart I'm a complete novice. Stands to reason, for when I think on it, I just discovered lately that I have one. But I'm quite willing to go down on one knee, my dearest Sylvia, or do anything else that's required."

"Oh, no, that isn't at all necessary, Roderick. Your proposal is imminently satisfactory."

"So—will you marry me?"

"You're certain that you won't at some later date mind about my mother?"

"Your mother has nothing to say to anything. Will you marry me?"

"Of course. It's what I've wished ever since I returned your snuffbox."

Had anyone been alert enough to interpret it, the cessation of melody in the drawing room might have served as a clue that some passionate lovemaking was taking place there. But there was no such signal in Lady Sylvia's bedchamber, particularly since no one besides Jenny and the butler was even aware that Mr. Chalgrove was on the premises. Therefore, the unwitting chambermaid who walked into the room carrying a scuttle filled with coal was not really to blame for the fact that, when she saw Lady Sylvia on the lap of some strange gentleman, kissing him as though that activity might never stop, she let the heavily laden scuttle drop through nerveless fingers. The resulting reverberating crash earned only the merest glance from Mr. Chalgrove. A master of aplomb, he carried on thereafter as before.

Jackson the butler stood, he thought, in grave danger of losing his position. For the second time, in defiance of her ladyship's order, a young gentleman had brushed on past him.

"You're a bit late," Jenny observed when Lord Dalton strode into the library where she sat reading. "Mr. Chalgrove arrived ten minutes ago."

"I know. I've been lurking, waiting for him to show up. By the by, where is he?"

"As far as I know, in Sylvia's bedchamber."

"Why, that sly dog!" He grinned.

She gave him a hard look. "Well, I must say you don't seem too upset by the fact your rival has stolen a march on you."

"Oh, I'm not." He pulled up a chair beside her and collapsed on it. "*Relieved* is the mot juste."

"Aren't you the same fellow who openly declared your intention of marrying my cousin Sylvia?"

"One and the same. But the situation's quite different now. I'm under no compulsion to wed. Thank God."

"I collect that out of loyalty to my cousin I should now take offense at your relief. But my curiosity has the upper hand. Just why were you under a compulsion—and what happened to it?"

"Well"—he stretched out his legs and yawned lazily—"for the first time in my life I was trying to please my parent. And let my case be a lesson to you, Miss Blythe. Never, never try and please a parent. It's a complete waste of everybody's time."

He went on then to explain his father's feigned illness and how he'd discovered he'd been hoodwinked. "So I no longer need to hurry toward the altar. The old fraud will probably outlive me. That is," he added quietly to himself, "if his increase in exercise doesn't bring on a seizure."

"I beg your pardon?"

"Never mind."

"Well, that explains a lot. I did think that for an acknowledged rake you weren't very skillful in your courtship. Still, if your heart wasn't in it . . ."

"If you're trying to insult me, you're wasting your time. I'm at peace with the world just now."

"I must say you look it. But just suppose that Sylvia and Mr. Chalgrove don't make a match of it, what then?"

"Don't be so negative." He frowned. "I have every confidence in Chalgrove. He's a most determined fellow. Always gets his way in the end. Does that

197

upset you? I realize he's no favorite of yours. As I recall, you even preferred *me* to him. Which sinks the poor cove past all redemption."

"I grant you I did feel that way in the beginning. But after he doused Lady Warrington with lemonade, it's amazing how Mr. Chalgrove's stock has risen." She grinned wickedly, and he laughed. "And as much as I'd like to see you squirm, I also expect his suit will prosper. There seems to be something in the air today. I strongly suspect that my cousins, Lady Claire and Lord Fremantle, are now betrothed. At least I saw them kissing shamelessly by the pianoforte."

"Did you, by Jove!"

"Isn't it famous? Aunt will need sal volatile."

"Hmm. Them in the drawing room and the other pair upstairs. That would appear to leave only us."

"Oh, well now, I don't like to boast—though of course I will when I go home—but I, too, have had a most flattering proposal."

She had his full attention. He sat bolt upright and glared. "Not that pup York-Jones."

"Why, yes, as a matter of fact."

"I'll kill him!"

"Why on earth would you do a shatter-brained thing like that?"

"Because I intend to marry you myself."

"You do?" She choked, then rallied. "In that case it's fortunate that I turned young Reggie down."

"Quite fortunate. Saves me a murder."

"But I don't understand." And, indeed, she did look dazed. "Didn't you just tell me, only minutes ago, that you didn't intend getting married?"

"No. You weren't paying close attention, a habit I trust you'll rectify once we're wed. I said I didn't *have* to marry. That's not at all the same thing as marrying to please myself, which I intend doing as soon as possible after we post the banns."

Jenny was beginning to collect her wits a bit. "And, when, may I ask, did you reach this startling conclusion? That we should wed, I mean."

"That's entirely the wrong question. For I couldn't get around to that stage till Lady Sylvia was disposed of. I would have hated to cause her any humiliation by appearing to jilt her. Far better that she jilt me. The question you should ask is when did I realize I was in love with you." There was a pregnant pause. "Well?"

"I'm sorry. I'm too busy trying to comprehend that you *are* in love with me. I haven't gotten around yet to wondering when it happened."

"Well, I'll tell you anyway. I've spent a great deal of time trying to puzzle the whole thing out, you see. For I don't mind saying, it took me by surprise."

"So I'd imagine."

"I collect I should have suspected when I kept thinking of another Percival daughter all the while I was actually pursuing Lady Sylvia. But since what I was thinking wasn't necessarily complimentary, I overlooked the symptom. I should have known, though. Then of course the clincher came when you coaxed me in off the ledge that infamous day. What a helpmeet to have, I told myself. No crisis too great. No hero too small. That's Miss Blythe for you."

She was regarding him suspiciously. "Surely you don't wish to wed me because I'm the only one who knows your guilty secret—that you're afraid of heights?"

His look was censorious. "I'll ignore that suggestion as unworthy of you.

"Of course, to be perfectly candid"—he grinned suddenly—"it wasn't the coaxing off the ledge part that was the clincher. It was the bit that followed on the floor of the landing that really cooked my goose. By the by, would you mind standing up for just a moment?"

"Not at all," she replied politely, and did so.

He took her in his arms. "I just wondered what it would be like to kiss a girl this tall while we're standing up. Should be a novel experience. I generally have to do a lot of stooping, don't you know. Well, here goes."

After a long, breathless interval he released her. "There now"—he grinned triumphantly—"that should take care of my fear of heights."

"Lord Dalton," she managed to gasp, "I do not intend to marry simply to prevent you from getting a crick in your neck."

"Seems a good enough reason to me. But let's try the sofa there for a change of pace. It could be even more satisfactory."

It was. So very satisfactory, in fact, that they remained oblivious when first Lady Claire and Lord Fremantle and then, a bit later, Lady Sylvia and Mr. Chalgrove came looking for Jenny to tell her their happy news. At least they were almost oblivious.

"I say," Dalton observed after they'd finally forced themselves apart. "Why do I keep having the feeling we're being watched?"

"A guilty conscience, perhaps?"

"My conscience is clear. My intentions are entirely honorable. You're the one with the problem.

I can't recall that you've ever said yes to my proposal."

"Yes."

This brief declaration called for another spate of lovemaking. At its conclusion, while Jenny smoothed out her crumpled gown to the best of her ability, Dalton found himself staring at the Romney portrait. "It must have been those Percival sisters that I felt watching us," he said. "I say, do you realize, my love, that your generation has outdone them?"

"You must be funning."

"No, I'm dead serious. It's true. Though it's undoubtedly immodest of me to say so, Fremantle, Chalgrove, and I are far superior catches to the ones they made."

"Don't be absurd." But she did look a bit smug as she played with the idea.

He had walked over to the mantle and was studying the portrait seriously. "Well," he concluded, "I must admit I can see what all the fuss and feathers were about. And, by Jove"—he reached up to touch the lady with the harp—"your mother's the loveliest of the lot."

"Thank you, but that's not my mother. Mama's holding the flute. She couldn't play a note, of course."

"But I thought the flute one was Caro."

"It is."

"Your mother is Caro? It can't be. Are you quite sure?"

"Of course I'm sure. I ought to know my own mother, for heaven's sake. Other people were always confusing the twins, of course.

"But whatever is the matter?" she asked anxiously. "You look as if you'd seen a ghost."

"My God!" he choked, and sat down suddenly. "What a rotten, miserable turn of events that is. Dammit, Jenny, this really is the outside of enough. I've just discovered that I'll be marrying to please my father after all."